AMISH STAR

BOOK 2

This Little Amish Light Series

RACHEL STOLTZFUS

COPYRIGHT

ISBN-13:978-1721985586
ISBN-10:1721985581

CONTENTS

ABOUT THIS BOOK

She's ready to leave the nest...but can she put her family, and love, behind her?

Gracie's voice is a gift from Gott, and she loves to sing. But as she steps into the spotlight, the strictures of her community's Ordnung become too much, and Gracie decides to leave. The two Englischers who discovered her talent agree to sponsor and mentor her in her new career, and Gracie wants to be happy, but is a life of fame and fortune really what she wants?

And can she truly leave her love, Daniel Byler, behind?

Find out in Amish Star – Book 2, the second book of the This Little Amish Light series. Amish Star – Book 2 is an uplifting, Christian romance about the power of faith and the gifts we all share.

PROLOGUE

Gracie and Abigail heard a scuffle and raised voices at the front door where services and the meeting were taking place. Moving to the entryway to the kitchen, Gracie gasped. "Mamm! It's the Wilsons!"

"Get back into the pantry. Close the door and don't come out until I say they are gone." Abigail hurried to the front door. "Deacon, why are they here? How did they find out where today's service was to take place?"

Eli raised his eyes to the ceiling of the living room. Sighing heavily, he spoke. "They saw all the buggies and came to the natural conclusion that, if other community members are here, Gracie would be here. Is she well away from them?"

"Ya." Turning to face the Wilsons, Abigail's face

transformed into a mask of pure anger. "And she isn't coming out until I tell her that it's safe to do so." Her voice developed a hardness that was rarely evident.

"But...I...we only wanted to talk to her! Just to see if there's any way she can compete without violating any rules or whatever..."

Deacon Eli sighed, feeling his patience rapidly disappearing. "Mister and Missus Wilson, we have told you many times that she cannot compete. There is the matter of her face being broadcast on televisions or whatever it's called. Then, we here don't believe in or allow competition. Third, she would be running the risk of becoming full of pride, which is a real sin. So...nee, she won't be coming out and she won't be talking to you. You are running a real risk by constantly trying to get in contact with her. Go. Now!" The deacon's voice bore a subtle growl, something that happened when he was angered.

"Please? She would have a real shot at winning the—"

"Missus Wilson, we don't care...she doesn't care about winning money. She has something here that is much more valuable. She has already told you, more than once that she isn't going to agree to compete. Do you finally understand?" Jon was absolutely fed up. Looking in back of him, he saw rooms full of picnic tables and people who were waiting to be served their lunch. "Now, if you don't mind, your presence here is delaying lunch. Why don't you understand the clues we are giving you and just go?"

Closed into the pantry, Gracie closed her eyes and tried to listen to what was being said. It wasn't too hard. Everyone who was waiting to eat had fallen quiet, making it easier to hear the voices in the living room. "Oh, please just leave! I don't want to talk… Wait. They need to hear it from me. Mamm, I'm sorry. I have to tell them." Opening the door, she rushed into the living room. Confronting the Wilsons, she spoke. "There is nothing you could say or offer to me that would induce me to change my mind. Now go!"

CHAPTER 1

Both Paul and Melody stood in the doorway, their mouths wide open. Melody slowly blinked, wondering at the new forcefulness in Gracie. Paul was unable to think, feeling real fear at the anger he felt rolling off the Amish people in the living room. "Uh, Melody..." He poked at her ribcage, risking making her mad as well. He licked his lips with a tongue that seemed to have become a mass of cotton. "Maybe we'd better..."

Melody turned and looked at him. Her eyes reflected the fear he felt. "Let's get out of here. We can't get them to listen to us." Drooping her head in defeat, she allowed her limp hand to run down the shoulder strap of her purse, looking like she was totally beat.

Paul turned, and putting a comforting hand on

her shoulder, led her down the porch steps. Inside the car, he was silent as he started the engine.

Melody closed her eyes, sighed and allowed her head to slump back against the headrest. As the car began moving, she stayed motionless...until they were just outside the Amish boundary. "Paul? Are you convinced that we have to give up on Gracie?"

"I don't want to! We have to be able to find—"

"...A way. Yes, we do. That little act I pulled back there? That was just a way of showing them that I'm going to stop. But we're not. Let's just go underground again."

"Again. Melody, you know that means it'll take even longer to get her to sign an agreement! And we have only eight weeks left before the show starts taping!"

"Paul. You haven't heard everything I'm thinking."

Paul looked more closely at his wife. She had never failed to surprise him and he realized she was about to do so again. Her eyes bore a familiar mischievous twinkle. "Uh, Melody, what are you thinking?"

Melody gave a wicked laugh from deep in her chest. "Your recording equipment, Paul. I want you to start carrying the smaller pieces with us whenever we come here. Because, when we are faced with resistance, we have to fight back."

"Okay, but you still haven't said what's on your mind. Out with it!" Paul waggled the fingers of one hand back and forth, signaling that he wanted Melody to say exactly what she was thinking.

"We're just going to have to be one step ahead of them. They aren't going to know we're here. We're not going to make contact with anyone. In fact, we aren't even going to be in plain view here. We're going to stay hidden. Then, we're going to catch Gracie when she's singing or even humming. She's the kind of singer that can't resist singing and it has to come out some time."

Paul laughed and snapped his fingers. "Oh-ho! I see what you're up to! What you want is for us to get a secret recording of her, wherever and whenever she happens to be singing. It could work…except that she was plenty angry back there. And so were her friends, family and those priests. She's really going to be on her guard, and that means she is going to hold back as much as she can on any form of singing. At all."

"Yeah. But, think about this. One day before long, she's going to forget. She'll be happy about something. Maybe about her boyfriend or something. And she's going to sing without remembering that she's not supposed to. We're going to be here every day that we can possibly get away from Philadelphia. We'll be hidden, close by wherever she is. If she's at home, we'll be somewhere that we won't be detected. If she's at the store, we'll be there. Or, if she's at that market, selling her stuff, we'll be there."

Paul rolled all of her ideas through his mind, thinking of every flaw he could find. "Hmmm... Well, okay... But..." Here, he looked at Melody. "If we try to hide out at their house, someone will see us. It's a quiet place, sure. But buggies and wagons are passing up and down that road in front of their house all the time. Maybe we should scratch the house as a hiding place. Look for other places, like when the teens hang out together, we can follow them."

Melody stifled a laugh, knowing that she would only anger her husband if she did giggle. "No, that won't work. For two reasons. First, when they get together, they aren't going to sing hymns. They're going to drink, go to the movies and just party like the non-Amish kids. Second, we'd get caught. They know what we drive."

"True. We'd have to rent a vehicle, one per week so they don't know what we'll be driving, if they look for us. Also, on the teen get-togethers, maybe they sing rock songs. Or something. We could get her then."

Melody tapped her lips with the tips of her fingers as she thought. "Okay, that could work. But we need to use a different rental company every week."

Paul continued to drive down the expressway as he thought. "We can do that. All of it. We're going to need to make a list of everything she does during the week. And you're going to color my hair. I'm going to shave and wear my glasses. You still have those brown wigs?"

"Yeah. We'll use them just as a way of not being recognized. But that's only if someone spots us. We don't want them raising a big old alert, telling her or her family that we're back. Or, nonviolence or not, they are going to run us out of that place, if they don't hang us first."

"I'll stop at the drugstore on our way home."

At home, Paul dumped the hair color box out of the plastic sack. He left it in the kitchen as he and Melody sat down for a discussion about the ways they could get Gracie's voice, legitimately or otherwise. "Okay, get a pencil and paper. Let's write down everything and come up with other ideas."

Over an hour later, they were done, confident that they could catch Gracie in song. "I want to make it my strongest recording equipment that I can conceal under a sweater. I'll use a special mic to catch her voice if we can't be too close to her."

Melody nodded. "Every time we're there?"

"Every single time. We don't know if or when she'll sing. Hopefully, she will. But we have to catch her whenever she does."

"And then?" Melody tipped her head.

"We're going to create a demo and send it to several local radio stations. I want them to hear how she sings. Then, they'll have to agree to allow her to compete."

"Well, we have a lot to accomplish, don't we? We'd better get busy. Chop, chop!" Melody jumped up, feeling energized.

৩৵৩

As Paul and Melody were talking, Gracie, her parents and everyone at the after meeting lunch were talking about the situation.

"Daed, I don't want to see them anymore!" Gracie's bravery and anger had evaporated, leaving her grasping for her courage and energy. She sat, hunched over and hugging her middle with both arms.

Deacon Bontrager kneeled at her side. "Child, listen for just a few minutes. We already have all the protections we can offer. You're doing everything right."

"Deacon, I don't intend to interrupt. But, even with all those protections and my sincerest efforts to stay away from those crazy people, they still turn up everywhere! And I can't even continue to participate with my friends and family, taking care of work, or having fun! All that's left is for me to stay at home, day and night. Become a hermit."

"Daughter!" Jon was about to scold Gracie when Deacon Eli intervened.

"Nee, Jon. As the subject of this couple's interest and pursuit, she is right to be frustrated. And she's telling no more than the truth. She's done everything exactly as we would have her act. And we're still no closer to banning these people from here than we were five minutes before they showed up here."

Jon backed down, keeping his words from slipping out. He sighed, knowing that everyone had done as much as they could. "So, what are we to do?"

"Keep doing what we're doing. We'll all protect Gracie. She's like a daughter for so many of our spouses. Gracie, keep doing exactly what you're doing. I understand my wife is covering for you at your baking booth."

"Deacon Bontrager, as it is, I'm not even going to my booth. Your wife is! And she is so generous for volunteering. I'm not leaving here when I get together with my friends. They have to sacrifice trips to theaters and restaurants so that I can spend time with them! They are suffering along with me!"

"Gracie, all we can do is just stay on the lookout for them. If any of us spots them, we are going to make them leave here. I think I speak for everyone when I say they've worn out their welcome for years to come."

Gracie sighed. She knew the deacon was right. "Ya, I know. Okay. I'll keep up with my usual efforts."

"As we all will, Gracie. You have nothing to worry about."

"Deacon, they aren't going to give up! Not until they get what they want. Or…" Gracie didn't know any fate terrible enough to force the Wilsons to stay away. She shrugged, feeling helpless.

Abe knelt at her other side. "Gracie, all of us will keep our eyes open. If we see them, we'll make them leave. We know what kind of car they drive. We know what they look like."

Gracie nodded. "Denki. Ya, that's true. I'm just tired of this whole mupsich mess."

Miriam sat in front of Gracie and took her hands. "Ya, we know that. You've been so gut about this. We don't mind staying here. We can find many places here that the Wilsons don't know about. They would have to travel down many roads unfamiliar to them to find you, ya?"

A small smile teased the side of Gracie's mouth. Looking at her closest friend, she nodded. "Ya, they would." She squeezed her friend's hand.

Abigail set her hand on Gracie's shoulder. "So, if you feel better, let's serve lunch. We have hungry people here!"

That night, Gracie sat, huddled in a warm coat, singing and drinking hot cocoa with her friends. At first, she hadn't wanted to go to the Sing, but Abe and her parents persuaded her to go. "They don't know about our Sings. They think we're all at home, getting ready for tomorrow."

"Okay, I'll go. But we close the barn doors when we start to sing!"

"We always do, when it's winter. Don't worry!"

Still, despite everyone's reassurances, the family

hosting the Sing was cautious. Sending several of their oldest sons and sons-in-law outside, they instructed them to be on the lookout for a green Subaru sedan. "If you see them, make them leave. We don't care if that means they realize she's here."

The sons all decided to split into two shifts so they could all get in from the cold occasionally.

The evening went uneventfully, with the teens enjoying hymn singing, snacks and hot drinks. Everyone knew that the men of the host family were walking around the property, waiting and looking to see if the Wilsons would have the temerity to show up.

On the way home, Abe drove, feeling confident that the two teams of men wouldn't miss the Wilsons should they try to stop Abe's buggy. "So, did the sing turn out the way you hoped?"

"Ya, it did. Denki." Gracie was happy, knowing that it would be nearly impossible for the Wilsons to get through to her. "I'm sorry for my tantrum this afternoon."

"Don't be. You had every right to be angry."

As Abe and Gracie were driving to Gracie's house, Paul and Melody were hidden from them. Rather than being within shouting distance, Paul had suggested that they take high-powered binoculars with them so they could stay farther way and still see their target. "It's a g-g-good idea that w-we decided t-to stay f-f-urther away." Melody gritted the words out, the bitter cold forcing her to shiver. Her teeth chattered, even though she kept her mouth closed.

"I told you to dress more warmly!"

Hot words of protest crowded onto Melody's tongue, but she kept her mouth shut. She didn't want Gracie to realize she was being observed. Instead, she glared at Paul. Feeling around her, she grabbed the thickly quilted jacket and stuffed her arms into it. Closing her eyes, she nearly groaned in relief.

"Okay, here they come. Because they don't know we're here, I'm pretty sure they're going to turn down that road right there; and yes, I was right." He raised the binoculars to his face and adjusted their focus. He continued to whisper. "He's stopped in their yard. He's kissing her...pretty involved kissing there! Okay, now, he's leaving and ready to go home. We'll move in a few minutes, Melody."

"Okay. Just don't let him realize we're still here."

Several minutes lapsed as they waited to make sure that Abe was truly going home.

"Okay. I think he's gone for the night. Let's go." Quietly, he led the way, trying not to step on crisp twigs. He brushed the dry leaves out of his way before moving forward, making the trip to the Troyer's home a long, halting one. Paul paused one more time, ascertaining which upstairs window might belong to Gracie. Seeing a dim, flickering light, he memorized its placement on the second floor. "Okay, she's in the room. Looks like it's five windows from the end of that hallway. Man, their houses are massive!"

Again, they crept cautiously to the road. Once they emerged from the heavy tree line, they sprinted toward the opposite side of the road. Here, they didn't need to be very careful. Instead, Paul bent nearly double, duck-walking toward first one bush, then another shrub. He was keeping them hidden so they were able to advance unseen to the house. Once situated under the window, they hid behind a large bush. "Don't poke yourself. If you do, try not to holler."

Now, they waited. Melody had pulled her knees to her chest for comfort and warmth. She listened for the sound of Gracie's beautiful, rich singing voice. Nothing. They waited for several minutes, their feet becoming painful blocks of ice. Cautiously, Melody nudged Paul. "Hey. She isn't singing, so I think we should go home."

Paul crept away from the house. Looking up, he saw that Gracie's bedroom window was now a dark square. "Yeah. Let's go."

Once back in their car, Melody let out a sigh, relieved that, in a few moments, they could begin to warm up again. "Wow. It's not even ten-thirty! They go to bed awfully early!"

"Well, wouldn't you if you had no TV, DVD player, computer or even a little tablet? I'd guess they have books, but not much else."

"Yeah, that could be the reason. Also, don't they get up pretty early?"

Paul thought of the research they'd done. "Yeah, before the sun even comes up. Speaking of which, we'd better get home fast. It's snowing. May not have any sun for them in the morning." He pressed down on the gas pedal, increasing their speed incrementally. Soon, they were back in Philadelphia, driving cautiously on roads that were snow-packed. Pulling into their garage, he whooped out a sigh of relief. "Depending on road conditions, I'd like to go back tomorrow, after our meeting. We really need to get that girl signed up. Or find someone who's just as good as she is."

The thought depressed Melody. She didn't respond back. Upstairs, in their bedroom, she got in bed and turned her back toward Paul.

"Hey, what'd I say?"

"You said something about signing someone else up, if we can find anyone who sings like her. I didn't like that."

Paul rolled over, his shock evident on his face. "Melody! We're signing people up all the time! We're saving that last slot for her, just in case they change their minds! I'm looking at the possibility that we won't be lucky enough to have that happen." Disgusted, he flopped back around, presenting his back to Melody.

The next morning, an Amishman, out hunting early, spotted foot-shaped depressions at the side of the road. Looking around, he realized they were adjacent to the Troyer home. He mentally marked their placement and, stuffing the plump pigeon into his sack, hurried off. At the deacon's house, he reported what he had seen.

Deacon Bontrager sighed. "Denki. I'll check it out in a few minutes. I'm headed to the store to buy some replacement parts for my plow and I'll pass right by their house."

"Won't they realize something is up?" The Amishman's eyes crinkled in confusion.

"Ya. They will, but the more they know, the better equipped they are to protect their daughter."

"Ya, true. Okay, I'll let you know if I see anything else."

"Ya, please do!" Drinking the last of his coffee, Eli buttoned his coat and, bracing himself, went outside.

❦

At the Troyer home, Eli sipped gratefully at the steaming coffee. "Denki, Abigail. Your coffee is as gut as my wife's. Ah, Gracie, there you are, child. Please sit."

Gracie closed her eyes, shaking her head. She knew what he was about to tell her. "They were here, weren't they?"

"Across the street. One of the men went hunting for pigeons for supper. When he came out again to the road, he saw footprints. Two different sizes. It didn't snow enough here to completely cover them. Either that, or the trees kept most of the snow from covering them. Did you feel anything?"

"Nee, I didn't. Abe brought me straight home from the Sing."

Eli grunted, becoming familiar with Abe's and Gracie's dating habits. "And you went straight to bed?"

"Well, to my room. I wanted to think and read for a while before I went to sleep."

"Jon, let's go outside and see what we can spot." Slurping back the last of his coffee, Eli donned his coat. Outside with Jon, he walked slowly, keeping his gaze pinned to the ground.

Jon's younger eyes spotted the same depression the Amishman had seen earlier. "There! Passing the crabapple tree and stopping…under Gracie's bedroom window." He looked up. "They must have wanted to see if they could see anything."

"Or hear. They must be getting desperate to sign her. I don't know if there's a deadline for signing contestants up."

Jon let out a sharp sigh of frustration. He rubbed the back of his neck, which had become stiff with tension. "Well, that's it. I was thinking of having her move to a room on the opposite side of the house."

"Jon, if I could make a suggestion. Let me pull a frolic together so we can build a taller wood fence for you. One with slats so they can't come into your yard."

"And a locking gate that swings in as well. Denki. I think we're going to have to do that. They are definitely persistent! Come in. Warm up with more coffee while we tell the women what we found."

Inside the house, Abigail moved the baking

supplies to the long counter as Gracie poured more coffee. "What is it, husband?"

Jon and Eli sat, waiting for Abigail and Gracie to sit as well. "Wife, Gracie, sit down, please. Gracie, we were told about footprints across the street. We found more coming into the yard and stopping under your window."

Gracie gasped, then began turning pink in anger. "How am I going to make them stop!"

"You're moving your bedroom to the back side of the house. Any room you want. Hopefully, they won't realize that and won't begin spying on you from the back of the house. Also, the deacon offered a frolic. To build a taller wood fence. One with slats that make it impossible for anyone to sneak into our yard. I hate to do it…"

"Do it, Daed, please. I truly hate feeling like someone's prey to be stalked." Gracie buried her head in her hands, unwilling to say anything more. She knew she'd get in trouble. She looked up. "Deacon, they aren't going to stop."

"Which means…what?" The deacon, well versed in the ways of teenagers, waited for her answer.

"That I'm going to be twice as stubborn. I am NOT going to give them what they want! I'm not interested in putting my face or voice on television. Ever!"

The deacon smiled. "Gracie, you are one of the more devout teens in our community. You've been raised well, and for that, I thank your parents. And you. Ya, keep holding tight to your decision because they will not stop. You have all of us to rely on when you begin to feel weak or tired."

"What day do you want the frolic?"

"Saturday. Sunday is not a meeting day, so everyone will be able to rest at home. I'll start the word going as I drive home, if you would start the word going in the opposite direction."

"Six days?"

"I'm sorry, Gracie. If we'd had this idea even yesterday, we could have set up a day during the week. Jon, Abigail, why not send her to stay with her friend's family until then?"

"But my baking!"

"Take your supplies and ingredients with you. Isn't Miriam's mamm a baker, too?"

"Nee, she quilts. Miriam bakes." Thinking of the suggestion, she smiled slightly. "Ya, it'll work. We'll do it the same way you and I do it here, Mamm."

"Deacon, would you go and ask her family if it would be okay? I don't want to leave Gracie or Abigail here alone, just in case."

"Gut idea. Ya. I will. Maybe Miriam will come by and take you there."

As it turned out, Miriam did come over. Helping Gracie take an overnight bag and several boxes with Gracie's ingredients and recipes, she chattered the whole time about the fun they'd have. "Gracie, I know you're coming over mainly because of those people not leaving you alone. But it's exciting! We can catch up on everything and maybe even come up with some ideas to frustrate those people from that show."

"I understand. And ya, normally, this isn't how things would be done. But, until the community can build a taller fence that they can't see through or get through…"

"Ya." Miriam's voice was soft in understanding. "This isn't the first time that I've been grateful I don't have your singing voice."

Gracie gave a soft smile. In the buggy, she looked all around the two of them. Not seeing anyone or sensing anyone, she sighed. "Miriam, I know my voice is Gott's gift. But this is the first time I wish He'd given it to someone else. Or that those people had never come to Crawford County."

Miriam's eyes rounded in amazement. Her mouth fell open. "I hope you haven't said that to anyone!"

"Nee. I know how much trouble I'd get into and I don't want that. Sometimes, I just wish I had any ordinary old singing voice. Or even one that's downright horrible!" Gracie's face was serious. "I even…"

"What?"

"Wonder if there's a way I could damage my voice so they'd leave me alone." Gracie dropped her head here, knowing she was saying something that the elders would strongly chastise her for.

Miriam gasped. "Gracie!" Thinking about it, she nodded. "I can see why you think that. I can't even imagine how it feels being stalked." Now, Miriam was watchful, her eyes sweeping all around so she could hopefully spot the stalkers. "Let's get home fast, just in case they're here."

"Nee, they aren't. I don't feel that creepy feeling." Gracie snorted. "But then again, I didn't feel it last night and they were here."

Hearing this, Miriam's eyes widened and filled with tears. She hurried the team along so they would get home faster. She felt a shivery sense of foreboding. She shivered as goosebumps prickled all over her skin. Soon, they pulled into her yard. Aiming for the lean-to, she and Gracie unhitched the horses, leading them into the barn. "Close and lock the door. I'll open the back one so we can see to get the horses fed and watered." A few minutes later, they were done. Gracie grabbed her bag and several full containers. Miriam grabbed the rest.

Miriam's mamm saw them from the kitchen. Hurrying outside, she relieved both girls of most of their boxes. "Inside! Miriam, you could have come in and asked me for help!"

"Ya, but we want to get inside fast. I'll tell you why in a minute." Miriam gasped, pulling in air as she put everything on the table.

Gracie put her burden down as well.

"Gracie, let me have your bag and I'll put it in the room across from Miriam's. Then, you'll tell me what prompted this change." Hurrying, she set the duffle bag on the neat spread and quilt. Downstairs, she poured hot coffee and set sugar and milk on the table. "Now, Gracie, please bring me up to date."

Gracie sighed as she added milk and sugar to her coffee. "Denki. After Abe took me home last night, I went upstairs. I read for a while before blowing my lamp out. I felt nothing, didn't feel like I was being watched.

"As it turns out, the Wilsons were spying on me across the street. They snuck *into our yard,* and hid behind the big bush under my window. What they were waiting for, I can only guess. Then, they left. A hunter, one of ours, spotted footprints under the trees across the street. They told Deacon Bontrager, and he came to our house. That's when Daed decided I'd spend a few days here until the frolic that the deacon is setting up."

"Frolic? What for?" Miriam's mamm was rightfully confused. "I haven't heard tell of anything."

"The deacon only thought about it this morning. He and Daed are letting all the families know. It's this Saturday. Everyone will help build a taller fence, one that has slats so nobody—like the Wilsons—can get into our yard."

"Ach! I see! Miriam, will you bake a shoofly pie for that day, please?"

"I'd be really happy to do so. It's a wunderbaar cause. I'm just glad we can help you out, even with these little things we're doing."

CHAPTER 2

B oth girls got started on their baking, grateful that the kitchen was so large. Before starting, they coordinated on the items they were baking so they wouldn't have to wait to turn the oven temperature up or down. As they worked, they chatted and giggled.

Working in her quilting room nearby, Miriam's mamm smiled. As she thought about the Englischer couple still stalking Gracie, the smile vanished. When she had been a young girl, she and her parents had lived the Englisch lifestyle. Her daed had decided not to be baptized and Margaret's mamm had already been pregnant with their first child, so she slipped away from the community with him. They got married by an Englisch minister. Several years later, they both realized they missed the discipline and

Plain life. A few years after Margaret was born, they returned to the community. After working hard to convince the elders that they were back to stay, they were baptized and welcomed back to the community.

Thinking back, Margaret remembered the extravagance of the foreign lifestyle. The music, styles, electronics, home decor, competition to one-up neighbors and friends and the all-out drive to win had eventually turned her parents away from their old life. *Now, I'm grateful that Mamm and Daed were open to telling me about that life. I wonder if explaining this to Gracie, her parents and the rest of the community would help.* Her fingers stilled on the hemming she was doing. She listed the pros and cons in her head. Seeing that there were more advantages to explaining what little she knew, she decided to discuss the issue with Saul, her husband.

At the end of the day, Gracie and Miriam sat in the living room, nursing sore feet and talking quietly. Miriam was confused when someone knocked on the front door. "Daed, are we expecting anyone?"

"Nee, not that I...wait! Let me get that. Saul thrust his *Amish Weekly* to the side as he hurried to the door. Peering through the peephole he'd added, he sighed with relief. "Gut. You can let him in. I thought it might be those foreigners."

Abe smiled as he stood just outside the door.

"Hello, Mister King. Is Gracie inside? I was told she would be staying here for a few days."

"Ya, come on in!" Swinging the door open, Saul accepted Abe's coat and hat. "Coffee?"

"Ya, that would be very welcome. I think we're going to have some snow again." In the kitchen, the three young people sipped their hot beverages and talked about the newest developments.

"So, the deacon and my parents felt that it would be best for me to stay here until a new fence is built this weekend. It happened so fast, I didn't have time to get word to anyone."

Abe shook his head. "That doesn't matter. What matters is that you are safe now. When your daed told me what the Wilsons had done... Well, let's just say my thoughts were very unchristian."

"All of us. Did you feel like they were spying on you?"

"Nee. Nothing. We'll all be at your place Saturday, working on the new fence. I think it's a wunderbaar idea. That they got right up to your house..." Abe shivered.

S aturday morning dawned clear, bright and cold. The breeze was nonexistent and, at times, gentle, which made the men grateful. As they sawed, took lumber to the perimeter of the Troyer property and constructed the fence, they talked about other ways of protecting the family and Gracie.

Deacon Bontrager, hearing the topics of conversation, stood. "Quiet! We need other topics of conversation, just in case." Here, he tipped his head toward the area surrounding the yard. Fortunately, he didn't have to worry about this. The Wilsons were stuck in Philadelphia, defending their decision to hold off on signing Gracie for the show. "Todd, we're waiting because Gracie is working to get the approval of her priests there."

Todd, the show's producer, scoffed. "Paul, the Amish don't have priests. They have elders, ministers, deacons and bishops. And you're going to be waiting for a very long time for her to 'get permission.'" He sighed, looking away from the Wilsons. "I think if you can let her know that we'd be willing to make any concessions necessary to make her and her *elders* happy, we can talk about that." Todd emphasized "elders" so Paul and Melody would get the correct term. "Now, what have you been doing about this girl and your other show prospects?"

Eagerly, Paul showed Todd the latest audition videos of the newest contestants they had signed. "And we're keeping up with Gracie on a weekly basis. If she's able to find a way to be allowed to record her audition tape, I think we'll be that much closer to success with her."

"So, Melody, update me again. How did you encounter this girl?"

Melody was ready with a whole bunch of lies. Licking her lips, she leaned forward. "Todd, we went to Crawford County on our day off. We were in that Amish community when we heard her singing. When I asked her to sing another hymn, she did. When I told her that we wanted to sign her for the show, she got scared. At first, she was doing everything she could to avoid us. But lately…well, I sort of sense that, maybe, she's changing her mind. Like, she wants to compete in the show. But she has to convince her elders to let her do so."

"Okay, when you've seen her recently, what has her attitude been like?"

"Friendly. Approachable. But, when she's with anyone, like her parents or the elders…even her boyfriend, she gets icy on us. Like she doesn't want anyone to know she's thinking of changing her mind."

Paul sat back, allowing Melody to work her magic on Todd.

"Huh. Well, when do you think she'll be ready to sign a contract? We have only eight weeks!"

Here, Melody hesitated. Her mouth widened into a slow smile as her eyes turned slightly flirtatious. "Todd, when have we ever let you down? We're getting used to a new culture, that's all. We're working on her. Okay, sweetie?"

Todd was secretly attracted to Melody, but hid it so Paul wouldn't figure it out. Leaning back, he gazed at Melody and Paul through lowered eyelashes. "Fine. Just deliver. Soon!"

In the car on the way back to their townhouse, Paul was silent. While he was grateful that Melody had won them a little more time, he wasn't so sure he liked how she'd done it.

"Hey, you okay?" Melody laid her hand on Paul's.

Slowly, Paul removed his hand from Melody's grasp. "Why'd you have to be so flirtatious back there?"

"Hey, I got a reprieve for us! It's just an acting job! Why? You jealous?"

Paul growled. "Yes! I am. You married me, not Todd."

"Because I love you, not him or anyone else. Let's talk more strategies for Gracie. I want to get her contract over to Todd as quickly as we can." Back in their house, she sat at the computer, browsing more websites about the Amish. "Hey, if those Amish kids in *Breaking Amish* can do so much, why can't Gracie?"

"Because, that show's not about the real Amish. Otherwise, we'd have signed her weeks ago."

"I think we should go back on Sunday evening. Catch her when she's coming home with her boyfriend and talk to her then. When she's not around those elders or her parents, she may be more willing to talk." Melody looked at absentminded Paul.

Paul was still pacing off his frustration with Melody's performance in the office.

"Paul? Paul? Paul!"

"Wha'? Huh?" Hands in his pockets, he spun around.

Melody sighed. With an exaggerated show of patience, she repeated her idea. "I think we should go to Crawford County and intercept Gracie while she's on her way home with her boyfriend on Sunday night. She might be more welcoming without any of the elders or her parents nearby."

Paul sighed, thinking. "Yeah. Okay. Weather permitting. And on one condition."

"Cool! What's the proposition?"

"Don't use your gender to get Todd on our good side again. I don't like that."

⚜

That Saturday, the entire community came together at the Troyer's to build the new fence surrounding their land and the house. By day's end, a new, much taller fence stood, painted white. Unlike the old fence, it had slats that repelled anyone who wanted to slip into the family's yard—say, to spy on someone.

⚜

Driving into the community early on Sunday evening, Paul hid the car in the hiding spot he liked so much. Grabbing their recording equipment, he and Melody, dressed much more warmly now, walked quietly to the Troyer's home—or what they thought was their home. "What! A fence? Let me check…" Pushing on the tall gate, Paul realized that it was locked on the interior side. "Mel, there's no way we can get in." Growling, he spit out several foul words. "Let's go hide. We'll catch up to them before they go inside."

Late on Sunday evening, after the Sing had ended, couples rode home in buggies. Abe and Gracie drove toward her parents' house. Driving up, Abe veered onto a narrow path.

"Gracie! Will you talk to us, please?" Melody ran through the snow and rested one hand on the side of the buggy. "I promise, if you let me talk to you today, I won't bother you again."

Gracie looked with alarm at Abe. "Abe, how…? No, Missus Wilson, I won't talk to you! I gave you my answer, weeks ago!"

Abe cracked the reins. In response, the horses bolted down the road and into a nearly invisible dirt lane. Gracie felt her back and neck muscles tensing up in response to the unexpected appearance of her stalkers. Gripping the seat and door of the buggy, she held on for dear life.

Again, Abe turned a sharp corner and the buggy's wheels responded by coming up slightly on the left side. As the wheels smacked the soggy ground, Abe stopped the buggy and hurried to unlock the back gate. Back in the buggy, he hurried it through and stopped right in front of the back porch. "Get in the house. I'll be right behind you!" Jumping back down, he ran to the gate, swinging it shut and locking it. Slipping in the mud, Abe catapulted himself up the back porch steps. Quickly pulling his shoes off, he slipped into the kitchen, depositing his muddy shoes on the newspaper sitting just inside the door.

"Daed! They're out there again! They tried to stop me as Abe was bringing me home!"

In response, Jon directed Abe to put his shoes on again. "Don't take your coat off yet. We're going to confront those two, then you're going to have some coffee and a slice of Abigail's apple pie." Jon and Abe disappeared outside.

Gracie stood just next to the window, trying to listen to the conversation. She caught a few words: "...weren't   here!   Don't...that   was...   Just want...sing."

"Her   alone!   ...To   sing   for   you...   Don't leave...sheriff."

Then, silence. Gracie backed away from the door as Jon entered with Abe right behind. "Daed, what happened?"

"They insisted they weren't here, sitting under your bedroom window last Sunday night. That they haven't been bothering you. I told them that we saw the footprints, not only across the street, but also in the flowerbed. And I told them that if they don't stop bothering you, beginning tonight, we will call the sheriff."

Gracie was about to ask what else she could do to reduce her visibility in the community.

Jon anticipated her question. Raising a hand, he spoke. "Nee, you've done everything you can do. Just live your life as normal, except for selling your baked goodies. That continues until they stop harassing you. Now, for that coffee and pie. Come, you two."

Abigail walked in as Jon was reassuring Gracie. "Abe? Thank you so much for helping her. I think that higher fence will do the trick. At least, when we're here at home."

Abe carefully moved one of the curtains to the side. "I don't see them. They would be mupsich to even try to get over that fence. Especially tonight."

In the kitchen, the four enjoyed slices of pie and hot coffee. "I saw who was in the road and I just cracked the reins. Gracie was brave, holding on. She told them 'no,' yet again and wouldn't listen to them."

"So, I just go about my days as I always have? Even though they're still out there?"

"Ya. I'm going to talk to Deacon Bontrager and see what he can suggest. I get the feeling that he'll tell me we're doing everything we're supposed to be doing."

"Jon, don't you have to work on that bedroom set? I thought you had that on your schedule for tomorrow." Abigail was confused.

"Yes, I do. But I'm going to get my foreman to get started on it with my best carpenter. Right now, it's more important for our family that I talk to the deacon tomorrow."

"Daed…" Gracie was about to continue until Jon raised his hand.

"Nee, daughter. Don't feel bad. I thank Gott that I have the resources I need so I can take care of you in the way you deserve. You did nothing wrong to deserve what's happening to you. I get the feeling those two"—Jon pointed toward the front of the house—"Are not going to stop anytime soon."

Gracie sighed. Drinking more coffee, she nodded. "Okay. Denki."

Abe set his coffee cup down. With a thoughtful look on his face, he spoke. "Gracie, you just came home from staying with Miriam until the fence was built. I have to go buy nails, bolts, nuts and stain tomorrow. What are your plans?"

"I also have to go shopping. But it's laundry day for Mamm. She can't go with me to the store, so I was going to ask Miriam."

"If your parents are okay with this, let me take you shopping. Do you want to go to the store here, or the Englisch store?"

Gracie sighed and grimaced. "I hate to do this, but I need to go to the Englisch store. The ingredients I need aren't stocked in our store. So…"

"That's okay. I'm in the same boat. I'll pick you up after breakfast. We should be one of the first few there, since they don't open until eight."

The next morning, Gracie climbed into Abe's daed's wagon. "Wow! Lots of room to bring supplies home! Are you going to buy the store out?"

Abe chuckled. "Very nearly. We need lumber not stocked here, as well as tools and other supplies. Do you have a lot of shopping?"

CHAPTER 3

In response, Gracie showed him a sheet of ruled notebook paper, filled up on the front and halfway filled on the back.

"Wow! So, it looks like shopping together was a gut idea in more ways than one!"

Gracie was looking all around them.

"You looking for them?"

"Ya. I don't feel like I'm being snooped on, so they may have gone home last night."

Abe's chuckle was forced. "Ya, with as cold as it was last night, anything else would have been stupid."

The couple chatted and laughed on their way to the Englisch discount store. Pulling into the parking lot, Abe decided to park his team and the wagon across several parking spots—a decision he would soon regret. Inside the store, each grabbed a cart or a trolley for their purchases. "Gracie, I'll come over here and wait, if you're still in line. You do the same if I'm still in line."

"Sounds gut. I'll see you in a while!" Gracie set off, knowing exactly where she needed to pick up the items for her planned baking. As she did, she was aware of more glances than usual from foreigners. Trying to ignore them, she softly hummed a hymn, forgetting her promise to herself, the elders and her parents. Picking up flour, sugar, spices, milk, juice and other items, she saw that her cart was filling up. She was unaware that, close behind her, trailed Paul Wilson.

Paul was dressed, not in his usual business apparel, but instead, in jeans, a long-sleeve sweater and boots. He wanted to blend in with the customers. In keeping with his attempt not to stand out, he had slipped a slouchy beanie over his deep-brown hair. He'd also slipped reader glasses on his face, which made him look more like a university student than a young businessman. He was wearing a dark pea coat, equipped with deep pockets. In one pocket, he'd slipped a small, high-powered recorder. To that was connected a sensitive mic, which was clipped to the top of his coat pocket. He followed Gracie from section to section, making sure he was staying well behind her. As he heard her beginning to hum, he discreetly removed the recorder from his pocket and set it so it would capture her voice while dampening the ambient noises all around them.

Gracie continued to hum, completely unaware she was being followed—her normal sensitivity to being observed was on break as she concentrated fully on her business. *Thanksgiving and Christmas are coming up. I'm going to have even more customers than usual, so I need to have all my supplies on hand for as long as I can.* As she kept this thought in mind, she hummed, slipping easily from hymn to hymn. Remembering some of the hymns from her Dolly Parton CD, she hummed a few of those as well. Thinking of "How Great Thou Art," she allowed her powerful voice to quietly go from low notes to higher, hitting all of them perfectly.

Behind Gracie, Paul was satisfied he'd captured several songs. Turning his recorder off, he slipped the tiny mic back into his pocket. Turning away from Gracie, he left the store.

I think that's it. I just hope I brought enough money with me. Nibbling her lower lip with worry, Gracie hurried to a cash register with the least number of waiting customers. She waited...and waited. Looking ahead, she saw that the customer being waited on had a huge sheaf of coupons, which the cashier was scanning one by one into the computer. *Oh, boy, why today?* Rolling her eyes discreetly, she shifted from foot to foot, praying that her perishable items would still be gut when she got home. Looking down the row of cash registers, she saw that they were equally busy. *Walmart has everything I needed, but it may not have been the best store to come to today.* Sighing, Gracie tried to hold onto her patience. Finally, it was her turn. She handed the few coupons she'd clipped over to the cashier and watched the running total anxiously. Seeing the cashier had hit the "total" button, she sighed in relief.

"That's one hundred forty-three dollars and sixty-seven cents, please." The cashier was a tall, attractive older woman with a friendly smile.

Gracie pulled one hundred fifty dollars out of her small purse, handing them over. "I'm relieved! I was worried that I wouldn't have had enough with me."

"You don't need to worry. I've waited on several Amish customers over the years. You're usually prepared with enough cash and your coupons. And, here's your change. I hope you have enough room in your buggy for all that!"

"I came with my boyfriend. We're in his wagon, because he had a lot of carpentry things to buy. Denki!" Looking all around her, Gracie spotted Abe just leaving the cash register as well. "You're done? Gut!"

"Ya. Lines are long and customers have tons of coupons to redeem today. Lunch? I'm famished."

"What time is it?"

Abe showed Gracie his receipt, which had the time stamped on it. "Nearly lunchtime. We can go across the street for burgers and fries, if you'd like."

"Ya, I'd love that!" Gracie's stomach growled in hunger.

⊛

Driving home, Paul called Melody, using his headset. "Hey, Mel! Good news! I found her. She was shopping at Walmart, of all places. She wasn't even aware that I was behind her."

"Did you get her voice?"

"Yes, I did!" Paul let loose a triumphant laugh. "She was humming several of her songs and I captured everything."

"Did that recorder and mic work?"

"Sure did! I had my earbuds in. Hey, thanks for suggesting I dress down a little. She didn't even notice me and I'm sure she looked right at me."

"Whoa! And she didn't recognize you?"

"Nope. Anyway, I'm going to have to work with the music program to remove all the noise. I want just her voice. Once I get that done, we're going to take it to several local radio stations and get her voice out there."

"I love this! Once she realizes just how much people love her singing, she'll have no choice but to agree!" Melody flopped down on the comfy sofa. "Are you sure she didn't know you were there?"

"Positive. Or she would have raised a major stink. She was pretty ticked off when we crashed their service or whatever it was."

"Thank God. Just get home. Travel safely. When you get here, I want to listen to what you got!"

"On my way, sweetie." Paul disconnected and gave full attention to the expressway. It was now dry except for accumulated snow and ice on the sides of the road. Before long, he was pulling into the parking lot of their complex. Grateful that they'd been given a day at home, he hurried inside. "Mel! Come here!"

Melody heard him close the door and call her name. Hurrying to the living room, she grabbed his coat and beanie, tossing them on the sofa to put away later. "Let me hear her! Now!"

Paul complied, hooking the recorder into their desktop computer. Adjusting the volume, he stood back. "Voila!"

CHAPTER 3   47

Melody covered her mouth with both hands, just listening. Her eyes slowly closed as she absorbed the pure notes emitting from Gracie's throat. "I don't understand without the words… Oh, wait! I've heard that one before!" She was now listening to "How Great Thou Art." "Oh, my God, Paul! She even does the non-Amish hymns! Are we still going to send this to local stations?"

"Yeah, why not? Once she and their *elders* hear just what a beautiful voice she has and how many people like her, they won't be able to keep her from participating. That's why we're doing this."

Melody clapped and squealed like a little girl, jumping up and down. "How soon can you clean up all that noise?"

"Uh, I expect it'll take me most of today, maybe some of tomorrow. But once it's done, we'll slap these little babies onto a demo CD and send them out."

☙❦☙

While Paul was cleaning the recording of all extra and unwanted sounds, Melody planned a quick trip to Crawford County. "Paul? I'm going to go and see if I might have any better luck with Gracie. Roads are clear, so I should be okay."

Paul looked at Melody. "Hon, you do know that we're both pretty much persona non grata up there, right?"

"Yeah. But, I figure that if I'm just straightforward and direct, I might be able to make at least a little progress. I'm not likely to come back with a signed contract, but if I even just get them to agree to think about it, I'll be happy with that."

As he thought, Paul drummed a pen repeatedly on the desk. "Well...okay. But if they get angry, you scoot on out of there and get back home. Right away! In fact, call me when you get back in the car."

"I will." Melody smiled. She loved this man so much!

"You'd better. I worry about you in the middle of hostile men and women. In fact, try to be home before it starts getting dark. I'll make dinner for us."

"Oooh, what are you thinking of?"

"Beef teriyaki."

"Wow! I'll definitely be home before the sun even begins to set!" Melody gave Paul a quick kiss, then left.

Once she arrived, Melody drove around, looking for any sign of Gracie or her family. Beginning to grow discouraged, she checked the time.

Driving her buggy home, Abigail and Gracie talked about the upcoming holidays. "Mamm, can we stop at the deacon's? I want to see if Missus Bontrager is still willing to help me out at the market." Gracie was conscious that she was imposing on the kindness of the other woman.

"Ya, that's a gut idea."

"I don't want to take advantage of her kindness. That's what I want to ask her."

"My Gracie. You've always been so considerate!" Pulling up into the Bontrager's yard, they both jumped out of the buggy. Gracie spoke with Mrs. Bontrager and was reassured that she wasn't imposing on her kindness.

"Gracie, we know you're still dealing with those people. And I won't rest easy until I know for sure and certain that they are gone! I'm happy to fill in for you."

Grabbing the older woman's hand, Gracie smiled. "Thank you so much. I just needed to be sure. I'm going to be sending more items to the market from here through Christmas and even the

New Year. We usually get more customers in those few weeks."

"Abigail, you'll continue to bring everything in?"

"Ya, I will. Gracie and I will load the buggy up. Then, at the end of the day, you'll give me her deposit bag and I'll load the empty containers into my buggy. And hopefully, this will end before too long!"

Gracie nodded fervently at this. "I wish it had never started."

Deacon Bontrager stepped onto the porch. "Gracie, Gott may have given this burden to you for a reason still to be clear to you."

Gracie nodded, feeling oddly apprehensive.

Abigail noticed her daughter's expression and hunched posture. "Daughter, are you okay?"

"Ya. Physically, that is. I just got a horrible feeling. Like something bad is going to happen." Her anxious gaze went from her mamm to the deacon and Mrs. Bontrager. "I just got this feeling." She looked all around them, as though she were looking for the source of her unease.

The deacon looked closely at Gracie. He knew she wasn't given to flights of fancy. "Child, why don't you do your work and just let Gott take care of things? Even if something does happen, you have all of us to help you through."

Gracie smiled, but only because she knew that it was expected of her. "Ya, I will, deacon. Denki." With her mother, she went into the yard and climbed into the buggy. She was quiet all the way home.

Abigail glanced at Gracie, wondering what she was feeling and what else could happen. "Gracie? Can you tell me what you're feeling?"

Gracie sighed. "It's hard to explain. One minute, we were making plans for selling my baked goods, and the next I just got this horrible, fearful feeling. Like someone's going to get hurt or something. And it won't go away."

Abigail now sighed. She began to feel the same sense of apprehension and worry. "Daughter, I think you're right. I'm going to say a prayer, asking that the burden be as light as possible for the recipient. I think you should pray as well."

Gracie nodded. Looking ahead, she silently pleaded to Gott, asking Him to keep the weight of the trouble as light as possible for the recipient. Little did she know she would soon be feeling even more pressure.

Over the next few days, Gracie quietly told a few of her friends about her feelings of foreboding. Abe was concerned and told her that she was not to be alone anywhere. "Be with me, your parents or even Miriam. I get the feeling you're going to learn something more from the Wilsons. Or hear something from them."

Gracie was leaning against a barn wall as they were spending time with other teens enjoying rumspringa. She was painfully aware that every parent of the teens in their group had forbidden them from leaving the community, because of the situation she was facing. "Ya, I'm already doing that. Daed won't even let me go to the store by myself anymore."

Abe sighed, rubbing his hands over his face. "I really wish they had not ever found our community. Ever."

Gracie rested her head on Abe's shoulder. "Same here."

◈❦◈

I n Philadelphia, Paul clapped his hands once in satisfaction. "Done! Melody!" He got up to go find her. He wanted her to hear Gracie's voice, now that he'd managed to remove all the other noises on the recording he'd made a few days earlier.

"Yeah, what is it?" Melody came out of the kitchen, wearing a snug pair of leggings with a long sweatshirt. Her feet were covered with thick socks.

"Man, you look cute like that! Little elf! Hey, I finished the recording, if you want to listen."

Melody's eyes widened. "That's like asking me if I want a piece of Godiva chocolate as you hold it just out of my reach! Of course I do!" She ran past Paul, into his studio. She danced in place impatiently, waiting for him to start the track.

"Introducing… Gracie Trayer, the Amish Songbird!" He got her last name wrong again.

Melody pressed her folded hands against her mouth, just waiting. As the sounds of her pure, young voice filled the room, she sighed and giggled. Once the last note had faded into nothingness, she whirled around, letting out a high-pitched squeal. "Oh, my God, it's perfect!"

CHAPTER 4

A few quiet weeks passed in Crawford County. Gracie, who was extremely busy with her holiday baking, was grateful for the respite—even if she didn't know how long the peace would last. As she was removing the last tray of Christmas cookies from the oven, she sighed, wiping beads of perspiration from her face. "That's the last one! Thank Gott!"

"You're done, too? I am and I am so grateful! One last market day before Christmas! Your daed and I were talking. We want to go through Lancaster on our way to your auntie's house. We thought we might stop in town, just to buy some things we need. So, save some money, because I know you've been needing more baking items."

"And shoes. And a heavier coat. I'd love to do that!"

The next day, Abigail and Mrs. Bontrager came back to the Troyer house, talking as they came in. "Ya, I'm just grateful that we've only had a few light snowstorms. I know several families here will be going away to see their families over the holidays, like you. Gut weather makes it much easier for you to do so. Gracie! Everything sold! You ran out of cookies and cakes in the middle of the afternoon!"

Gracie's jaw dropped. "And that was with baking so much more! Mamm, I think I'm going to have to add another baking day to my week."

"Ya! Me, too! I think we're going to have to think about moving our baking into a building nearby. Doing our baking, storage and selling from there!"

Gracie gasped. She had long wanted to do this! But her mamm had always been characteristically cautious. "Mamm! Are you serious?"

"Very much so. After the holiday is over, you, your daed and I are going to sit down and go over our weekly earnings, our savings and finances. We're going to see if, financially, we can do this."

Gracie squealed, covering her mouth with both hands. Before she started running around the kitchen, she slapped both hands onto the back of a chair. "Finally! Mamm, we've been ready for this for so long!"

A fter Gracie and her parents had left for Lancaster, Abe buckled down with his carpentry work. Knowing he needed to fill the hours, he was grateful for his trade. Right before Christmas, he and Ben went into town to buy lumber and supplies that had run low. Waiting in line in a local lumber supply store, he shook his head, thinking he was hallucinating. Focusing on the song coming from the speakers, he realized he was hearing Gracie's clear voice as she hummed a hymn. His shoulders, neck and back grew hard with tension and anger. Hearing the DJ's patter when the song ended made him even angrier.

"Everyone, you've been blessed during this holy season to hear the voice of the Amish Songbird. From what we know, she is almost local. Let us know if you want to hear more of her beautiful voice—we have a few more tracks."

Abe turned, looking at Ben. "Daed, that was Gracie!"

Ben's eyes were wide. "How? Did she finally give in?"

"Nee, Daed! All along, she has been refusing to give in to them. I just hope she and her parents aren't hearing this. We need to talk to her…and to Deacon Bontrager."

In Lancaster, Gracie and her family had heard the track. They had stopped at a local Cracker Barrel for lunch one day. As they were eating, Abigail and Jon heard Gracie's voice issuing forth from the overhead speakers. Jon's fork dropped. He looked at Gracie and Abigail. "Daughter. That's you!"

Gracie was confused. Looking at the direction of her daed's finger, she realized she was hearing herself. Putting her fork down, she pushed her plate back. Her appetite was ruined. "How? When did they get this?" Hearing "How Great Thou Art" as she had hummed it, she remembered being at the Englisch discount store. Her eyes widened, allowing tears to fall. "That's when I was shopping for all the baking things I needed. They had to be there, only I didn't realize it. I didn't even see them. Daed, Mamm, I am so sorry!" She got up and ran to the ladies room, Abigail close behind.

"Daughter, you didn't know. We'll call the bishop from your uncle's phone. We'll let him know what we heard and how it must have happened."

Wiping tears from her face, Gracie nodded. She

knew that was all they could do. "Ya, that's fine. I just hope I won't be in trouble."

"Why would you be? You didn't do this knowingly. They took advantage of you."

The remainder of the holiday had taken on a pall for the Troyer and Lapp families. As soon as Gracie and her parents arrived at her uncle's house, Jon called the bishop and left a message for him to call. "Something happened. It has to do with that couple chasing after Gracie."

Receiving the message, the deacon called back at the number Jon left. "You heard what? Gracie's voice on a recording? But...how?"

Jon explained the whole issue. "She says she's never agreed to record anything for them. She never gave them permission. But somehow, they found her and managed to record her. Deacon, she is right upset."

"She won't be in trouble. Those people, though—the ones who have been hassling her—the blame is all on them. Tell Gracie, from me, that she should relax. She has done nothing wrong."

Even after hearing what the deacon had said, Gracie was unable to recover her usual high spirits. Once they returned home, she decided that she still could not chance being seen in public, just in case the Wilsons decided to show up. Abigail agreed. "We don't know when they'll pop back up. Daughter, you let me deal with them. You just stay as far away from them as you can."

"That's no problem! If I were to see them, I don't know what I would do or say."

Driving to the Bontrager's, Gracie and Abigail explained the whole situation. "So, we think it's best for her to continue avoiding the market until we know for sure and certain that those Englischers are gone for gut. I hope you don't mind."

"Nee, I don't. Ever since I retired from teaching, I've been a little at loose ends, and working at the market gives me a chance to give back."

The deacon joined the women. "Gracie, look at me, please. You don't have anything to worry about. You haven't violated the Ordnung. All you need to do is just don't let them get to you. And I know that's easier said than done." He sighed. "I think it's time to get some of the men to watch the roads coming into our community. But we're going to have to wait until this storm we're expecting blows out. Ach, the wonders of Englisch weather forecasting! At this moment, that's the only gut thing I see coming from them. Anyway, we are going to try and stop the Wilsons from coming here and bothering you."

"Denki. I appreciate you telling me that I'm not in trouble."

"Abigail, what was Gracie's voice like on that recording?" The deacon was curious.

"Beautiful as always. But a shock, when we realized the source of her singing. She told us she has never given them permission!"

"And I believe you. Just keep exercising the usual precautions until we know they're gone."

Gracie nodded. "I will."

☙❧

The next day, Abigail was busy at the market. Gracie, at home, baked more goods to be frozen for the next week.

☙❧

Abigail, arranging her remaining baked goods looked up, sensing trouble. Her lips tightened as she saw the Wilsons approaching.

Paul and Melody strode up, hands in their pockets, smiling as they looked at Abigail. "Did you like the recording?"

Abigail dropped a cupcake she was holding. Not caring that it had landed on top of two other cupcakes, she glared at the couple. "Do you understand that you have frightened my daughter? She refuses to sing in public! Just leave her, and us, alone!"

Paul smirked. "Missus Trayer, you should just realize and accept the inevitable. Your daughter has a beautiful voice, one that is unique in girls her age. We're leaving here today, but we aren't leaving for good. She has a real shot of winning that show. If she does, she brings home over two hundred thousand dollars. Can you imagine what you and your family could do with that? I'm sure you're doing really well now, but if you have plans..."

Abigail clamped her lips shut. *The bakery.* "Just get...out...of...here. Now!"

The disgusting smirks returned to Melody's and Paul's faces. Turning around, they waved as Abigail stood stiffly behind her table. "See you!"

"Abigail, I saw everything. They don't know that I'm married to Eli. I'll tell him just what they said. They admitted to making that recording!"

"Ya, they want to scare us. I'll tell Jon and Gracie just what happened. I promise."

That night, a stiff wind and snowstorm blew into Crawford County. Everyone who knew it was coming had already taken all the precautions they could. Livestock were snug inside warm, fragrant barns. Families had long since made kinder come into the house. School was postponed until the first gut day when families could navigate the roads to the schoolhouse.

The Troyers took the storm's arrival and used it to their advantage. As Jon had promised, they went over the finances, prospective costs and benefits to the family if a separate bakery was constructed. Looking at their savings accounts and bank balance, they determined that they could afford the lumber and other supplies. "How much do you think ovens and refrigerators will cost?"

"I've been looking through newspapers and the Amish Weekly. I found a few possibilities. Used, but in gut condition. One is in almost-new condition, according to the seller. That's the oven. We'll also need a counter, refrigerated display cases and generators. I'm looking through regular newspapers for those items. But, since we'd ask for help in raising the bakery, I expect that, for the cost of the lumber and other supplies, we would have quite a few dollars. I was also thinking that we could just build it on our land. So, that would save quite a few dollars. We wouldn't have to buy a lot. We have a large amount of property here."

"Hmmm. That's a right gut idea. We don't have crops, so we have all that land just sitting there. I'd have to talk to the deacon and see what he thinks. But I don't think he'd say no."

Gracie simply allowed her gaze to move from Mamm to Daed and back again, listening the whole time. "Mamm? I have a question and a thought. You and I are already working as fast and hard as we can to keep up with the demand for our baked items. Once we move into a bakery, we're going to be just as busy, ya? So, I am thinking we should hire at least one girl to help with the baking. Once the bakery opens, someone's going to have to be up at the front, selling to customers and making sure the cases are fully stocked."

Abigail was silent, just thinking. "That's a gut point, Gracie." She jumped as a particularly loud shriek of wind buffeted the large house. "My! That wind is strong!"

Jon got up, stretched and looked outside. "Man, it

is coming down! I estimate at least three inches, maybe more!"

Gracie laughed. "It's ironic! I hope this storm makes it impossible for the Wilsons to come back here, for several days."

Abigail and Jon looked at each other, nodding.

❦

In Philadelphia, the Wilsons were definitely stuck inside their warm townhouse. Paul looked outside, turning on the outdoor light. "Whoa! The car tires are almost covered…whoa!" The power had gone out. Moving slowly, he went to the kitchen table, where they had been told to keep lighters, candles and flashlights. Picking up the camping lantern, he turned it on. He squinted against the sudden light, moving quickly to set it on the fireplace mantel. "I hope the power comes back before too long. Did you pull the blankets out?"

"Over there. We'd better put on extra layers of clothing." She grabbed sweatpants and put them on over her snug yoga pants. Over her long-sleeved sweater, she put a heavy ASU sweatshirt.

Paul did the same, donning a pair of sweatpants over his jeans. The sweatshirt covered his flannel button-down shirt. "Here, put these on." He tossed a pair of thick, woolen socks to Melody, who slipped them on.

The storm blew through that night, all the next day, that night and finally blew itself out on the second day as it lumbered toward New England. Jon had tied long lengths of clothesline between the back door and barn. He used this as a way of finding the barn and house as he tended to the livestock. Gracie helped him; his workers were stuck at home, unable to come in to work. While the family was waiting for the storm to end, they continued making plans for the new bakery.

"As soon as we can, we can set stakes into the ground for the bakery. If we're able to get to meeting this Sunday, I'll speak to Deacon Bontrager about our plans." After several hours of discussion, planning and looking at dollar figures, the family had figured out that as long as they were cautious with funds and purchases, they could make the bakery work.

For Gracie, the storm was a welcome reprieve from her fears of encountering the Wilsons and trying to stop them from conning her. She felt almost happy again. Even so, she still felt violated because of how Paul had obtained his recording of her voice.

❦

U p in Philadelphia, Paul and Melody endured three days without power. They quickly realized that without power they couldn't even heat ramen noodles. So, they subsisted on things they didn't need to heat up. They poured the milk into the sink, knowing it had gone bad. And, being cooped up inside for seventy-two hours, they began to get on each other's nerves. Melody stomped out of the living room and into their bedroom, slamming the door shut after a loud argument with Paul. As she flounced onto the bed, she muttered several swear words, assigning several colorful descriptions to her husband. Looking up, she realized the light had changed outside. Running to the window, she looked outside. "It's stopped snowing! Hallelujah! We're going to live!" She failed to take into account that it would take time for the electric crews to get to the section of the electrical grid that powered the electrical line to restore the power.

CHAPTER 5

For two long, cold and dark days, Melody and Paul coexisted in their townhouse. As the hours wore on, they began to get on each other's nerves. By the evening of the first day after the storm, they were both sniping and arguing at each other. "Ahhh, okay, fine, Melody! We don't know when the power will be restored, all right? We can't use anything from the refrigerator. It's gone bad! So get your craving for ice cream outta your head and satisfy yourself with cookies or fruit or something."

Melody, never very reasonable in the face of a crisis or unexpected event, was whining. "But I want ice cream! It's not fair that this stupid storm knocked power out!"

"Melody! Shut up! No, it isn't fair! But your

whining is getting on my last nerve!" Paul stalked down the hall and burst into his office. Just before he slammed the door, he yelled at Melody down the hallway. "If you're going to come in here to whine more, I won't listen. Get it out of your system by yourself." BANG! The door shut with a resounding, somewhat satisfying slam. In response, the couple above them stomped loudly on their floor. Paul, hearing the three dull thuds swore loudly and colorfully.

Back in the kitchen, Melody's mouth hung open at the slam of the office door. Then, she returned to her whining about the lack of perishable foods. When Paul's sulk session went on well into the evening, Melody gave up on getting his company for the evening, let alone the night. Stomping over to the linen closet, she pulled out blankets and a set of sheets. She threw them on one end of the couch. Grabbing a sheet of paper and a pen, she scribbled a note: You sleep on the couch tonight. In their room, she pulled on a long-sleeved T-shirt and sweatpants. It wasn't a sexy look, but she wanted warmth more than sexiness tonight. Besides she was royally ticked at Paul. After brushing her teeth and washing her face, she locked the door to their bedroom and flopped into bed.

In his office, Paul yawned. He had been hanging out, browsing the internet on his phone. Realizing that it was running low on its charge, he shut it off. In the living room, he saw the terse note and bedding. Frowning, he went to the bedroom, finding the door locked. Growling under his breath, Paul made up a bed on the long sofa. About to undress, he changed his mind, just taking his shoes off. Pulling the covers over himself, Paul sighed, hoping he'd be able to sleep.

Several hours later, Paul squinted at the sudden glare of light in the living room. "Wha'? Who forgot to turn—? Yes! The power's back!" Looking at his watch, he saw that it was time to get up anyway. Bypassing the bedroom, he used the powder room to do his business, pulling a new toothbrush out from under the sink.

In the master bedroom, Melody woke up, stretched and realized it was morning. She forgot about the power outage that had lasted most of the previous day. Wandering into the bathroom, she tried to take a shower, but when the water stayed cold, she began whining under her breath. "Guess I'm just going to have to stink! That should make Paul happy."

In the kitchen, both Melody and Paul stayed stubbornly silent as they looked for nonperishable things to eat.

※

I n Crawford County, the Amish families were better situated to weather the severe storm. Relying on their gas generators, they were able to keep their appliances running, which meant life went on almost normally. The night the storm became severe, everyone went into "storm mode," meaning nobody left home except to take care of the livestock. Carpenters told their workers to stay at home because it was too dangerous for them to be on the road. By the time the storm ended two days later, snow had piled up in yards and against buildings three feet high. Whole families went out to shovel snow. Knowing the moisture would be welcome when they started planting crops in the spring, farmers didn't worry about the heavy snow blanketing their fields.

Inside the Troyer home, Gracie and Abigail baked while Jon worked on small carpentry projects he had been delaying—making small, wooden animals for his grandchildren.

Inside the house, Gracie hummed, sang and baked, feeling the heavy burden of apprehension and outright fear leaving her body and mind. Knowing the Wilsons could not navigate the roads to snoop on her or steal her voice in recordings, she sang at full voice as she worked.

Jon and Abigail smiled, grateful to Gott for Gracie's temporary reprieve. They knew that once the snow melted, the Wilsons would come back around, attempting to get Gracie to change her mind. Looking at his wife, Jon whispered to her. "We need to remind her tonight after supper that they will come back. Then, she can be ready to watch for them."

"Ya, I know. But give her these few fear-free hours. She needs that. And we need the sound of her voice."

Jon nodded. "Ya, we do."

As planned, Gracie's parents sat down with her after supper. Jon cleared his throat, which told Gracie that he intended to talk to her about something serious. Swallowing hard, she stiffened her back. "What is it, Daed?"

Jon cleared his throat once again. "Gracie, we have had a few blessed days of reprieve from the Wilsons. Which means this storm we had hit Philadelphia as well. But you know, once the snow melts and they dig their car out from the drifts, they will be back, ya?"

Gracie sighed. "Ya, Daed. I know. I was just enjoying the few days of relief without having to worry that they would jump out from behind a barn wall or something, trying to make me agree to that stupid television show."

Abigail sighed, leaning close to Gracie. "Gracie, we don't want to ruin your happiness of the past few days. We just want you to remember…"

"That they are still out there. Ya. I know. How long do you think they'll be snowed in?"

Jon shrugged. "Who knows? It depends on how much it snowed in Philadelphia. Maybe, if the snow melts enough in the next day or two, I can go to town and find a television set or radio and listen for the report."

Jon would be spared that trip. Minister Dan Summy came by the house late the next morning. As he smiled at Jon, his face was red from the cold.

"Dan! What brings you here? Do you need help at your house?"

"Nee, denki. We just came back from Philadelphia. If you think we got it bad here, you should see it up there!"

"Wait. Let me get Gracie and Abigail." Jon called to both women and told the minister that they also wanted to hear his news.

"Ya, I can see why, under the circumstances. Gut

morning, Missus Troyer, Gracie. I hope you got through the storm okay?"

"Ya, we did. How about you and your family?"

"We were in Philadelphia when it hit. We had to find a hotel pretty fast—we had gone so Thomas could complete his follow up appointment to treat his scoliosis. We were stuck there until this morning, early."

Gracie held her hands tightly together. "Mister Summy, how much snow did you get up there?"

"We got well over a foot here. Up there, it snowed a gut two feet or more. Our driver has a big truck. He equipped it with a snowplow on the front. And that's the only way we got home! Nothing is moving. Nothing!"

Gracie closed her eyes and folded both hands over her mouth. "So that means…"

"That those people who have been bugging you— can't get out. For at least the next three or four days. Or more. They drive a smaller car. Jon, I can promise you that their car is buried in drifts and straight snowfall. They will be fortunate to find their car in the same condition they left it in."

Abigail's forehead crinkled. "What do you mean?"

"The snowplows are going to try and get onto the roads today. If they park on the street, then that means their car has a gut chance of being damaged just because it can't be seen. But, if they are fortunate enough to have a parking garage to park in, then as soon as the roads are clear…"

"Then, they'll be back."

"Ya, exactly. I give them three days of getting out of the city."

"Three days." Gracie was thoughtful.

"Jon, I had an idea. I know it may not be ideal. Gracie, you bake, ya?"

"Ya. Why?"

"I want to talk to you and your parents about the possibility of ferhoodling the Wilsons by staying with a different family. So they don't know where you are. If they can't find you…"

Gracie looked at her parents. "Mamm? Daed? What do you think? I could ask Miriam again."

Jon looked at the snow-covered road. "Let me think about it, Gracie." As he looked outside, a memory of the recording of Gracie humming came back to him. He sighed.

Gracie mistook his sigh for not wanting to let her go. "Daed, I'll be fine. I promise."

"Nee, Gracie. I was thinking about that recording. You sounded so… "

He paused, not wanting to give a reason for any vanity to rear its head in Gracie's spirit.

"Jon, I haven't heard that recording. Did it sound anything like Gracie's natural voice?"

Jon nodded. Catching a look from Abigail, he coughed and changed the subject. "What else, other than staying elsewhere, would you recommend for Gracie?"

"That's all. We can't do very much else."

Again, Jon sighed. "Ya. Gracie, you can stay with Miriam, *if* her parents agree to this plan. I pray we won't have to be moving you from home to home. That wouldn't be gut for your spirit or for your business."

Now, Gracie sighed. "And here I was, enjoying a reprieve from those people." Uncharitable thoughts invaded her mind.

Minister Summy noticed the change in Gracie. Blessed with a high sensitivity to the feelings of others, he realized what was happening. "Gracie, don't allow the devil to take over your thoughts. Remember, the Wilsons are just doing their work, as dishonestly as they have conducted themselves around you."

Gracie gritted her teeth. "Ya. I understand, Minister. But they have totally turned my life upside down! I can't go to market with Mamm. I only go shopping with Mamm or Abe. And they have things of their own they need to be doing. And the Wilsons have just been so…selfish!"

"You have been through the wringer. I tell you what. How long will it take you to work through this anger you're feeling?" Minister Summy had a relative who had moved to live among the Englisch. He was highly perceptive and able to use some of the psychology that his relative used with his clients.

Gracie huffed out a laugh. "I don't know! A week? A year?" She crossed her arms over her stomach, wanting to hold in the rage.

"I'll give you the rest of this day to work through it. Indulge it. Imagine the worst punishments possible for the Wilsons. The worst outcomes for everything they could attempt to do in their lives, whether it has to do with you or not. And, when you blow your lamp out tonight, you have to stop indulging. Give it up to Gott and let Him deal with it."

Gracie looked at her parents, then at the minister. "We've never been told we can do that!"

"That's because we don't like anger as an expression. I have a relative who is now Englisch. Now, believe it or not, gut things come from the Englisch sometimes. His education in psychology and the study of the human mind is one such thing. I have learned a lot by watching how he works with his clients. Anger is an emotion that we honestly feel when something doesn't go as we wish for it to go. You, more than any of us, have the right—ya, the *right*, Gracie—to feel and express your anger. I'm not sure what any bishop would say about what I just said. But I want you to begin to move ahead and have the tools you need to deal with the Wilsons, ya?"

"Ya. I promise. Feel my anger and let my imagination go wild until I blow out my lamp, then it's over."

"Exactly. Also, start asking your friend about staying with her and her family until this whole sorry episode comes to an end."

"I promise. I will."

"And bless your family with your singing. Again, keep that within the four walls of your home."

"I will. Denki." For the rest of that day, Gracie did as she had been told to do. Once the minister left, she allowed herself to honestly feel her anger. As she finished her baking, she muttered her feelings and thoughts about the Wilsons, imagining that they lost their business with the reality show. *I hope you become homeless, living on the streets. No more car, no more fancy clothes or jewelry. And you can't even do anything about me refusing to go on your mupsich show.*

As Abigail worked on supper, she heard snippets of what Gracie was thinking and saying. Not sure she should encourage Gracie, she stayed quiet. Then, her own anger was kindled, thinking of all the freedom Gracie had been forced to give up. She spoke up to one of Gracie's mutterings. "Ya. I agree with you, Gracie! I want them to be homeless and helpless, too!"

Gracie looked up, her mouth falling open. "Mamm! Really?" Her voice went up in amazement.

"Really, ya, Gracie. You have been forced to give up so much of your freedom because of them and it *makes me mad*!"

Gracie was still. Then, looking straight into Abigail's eyes, she spoke. "I want them to be fired from their jobs for what they did to me. Then, I want Englisch law enforcement to arrest them…"

Abigail picked up on Gracie's words. "… And spend the rest of their lives in prison."

Gracie finished her baking, continuing to talk with Abigail about everything bad she imagined happening to the Wilsons.

"And I hope, as I am putting supper in the oven, that one of those snowplows will smash into their car so it is destroyed. And, even more, they can't afford to buy a new one! And that this whole sorry mess ends."

As Abigail was talking, Jon came in. Hearing what the two were saying, he grinned at them. "You have permission until bedtime. I am not going to join you."

"Husband, why?"

Jon sent a dark look to her. "Because my imagination goes into places that are just too dark."

CHAPTER 6

"That…" Gracie dragged a deep breath in. Moving her baking pans and dishes to the sink, her hands trembled. "That is scary. I think I'd better just deal with my anger quietly. I'm sorry, Daed, Mamm."

Jon caught Gracie's upper arm in his hand, holding on lightly. "Nee, daughter, you should deal with it in the best way you can. If you allow it to stay inside you, it'll fester like a bad cut. I agree with Minister Summy. I just feel as though there's so little that I can do to protect you. And that's extremely frustrating for me."

Again, Gracie licked her lips, feeling as though she needed an entire vat of water just to get moisture back in her mouth. "Sh-should I be quiet about this when I'm around my friends? Or Abe?"

Abigail looked at Jon, asking him to answer.

Jon sighed. "It's best for you to share it only with Abe. I would imagine he feels the same frustration I'm feeling. And as far as sharing with your friends, I'd be careful about that. You may wind up in trouble with some of the more conservative members of our community."

"That's true. I'm glad I asked. I really need something to drink!"

"Coffee. I'll make a pot right now. This has unsettled all of us. Besides, I need to get started with supper, Gracie. I need your help."

Gracie quickly washed her baking items, cleaned the kitchen counter and table and, as she drank her hot coffee, helped Abigail with supper. As they worked, Gracie and Abigail talked quietly.

"Mamm, have you felt the same frustration as Daed?"

Abigail sighed, boiling the pieces of chicken she planned to use for the potpie she had decided on. "More like helpless, I think. And that's frightening, even though you're almost an adult. Ever since you and your siblings were born, I've wanted to be there to protect you from the bad things of this world. And usually, I could. Sometimes with your daed's help. But now... I know so little of the Englisch entertainment world. I don't know *how* to protect you from anything those two could do. And I think that's where everyone's frustration comes from."

"Mamm, do you remember that Abe and his daed went to the library and got help on the internet? They learned so much about those reality TV shows. I think we should do the same thing. Maybe this Saturday, if the roads allow us to go into town? What's that saying about being armed or forearmed?"

"Forewarned is forearmed. And that's true, ya. If we finish everything, then we'll go. Maybe your daed will go with us as well."

Gracie nodded quickly. "Ya! Because, if the roads clear for us, they'll clear for the Wilsons, too."

Abigail grimaced. "I really don't like thinking about them." Thinking about the Wilsons gave Abigail's potato-mashing additional energy.

"Mamm! Be careful or you'll turn the potatoes into mush!"

Abigail set the masher down and rested both hands on the counter. Her head dipped down toward her chest and she exhaled. "Denki. We'd better stop talking about them or I'll ruin supper."

"Ya. I know what you mean." Gracie tasted the gravy for the chicken potpie. Satisfied that it was spiced correctly, she moved the frying pan to the back burner and quickly made two crusts for the potpie. Used to helping her mamm from the time she was little, she quickly assembled the pie and set it into the oven. "I keep thinking about the bakery. I'm so excited!"

"Ya, your daed got everyone to agree to help in raising the building for the bakery. We're settling on a week from this Saturday, weather permitting."

"Who are we going to hire to help with baking?"

"I was thinking of Miriam and one other woman. You and I would change off on the baking and managing the front of the bakery, working with customers. And, nee, the Wilsons will not be allowed to enter."

Gracie nodded in agreement. "Ya, they've only ever been a problem for us here."

❦

Paul came into the townhouse, bundled up and panting. He tossed a borrowed snow shovel to the side and collapsed onto the couch. "Man, digging the car out is hard work!"

Melody looked at him, seeing Paul's bright-red nose. Gasping, she got up and poured a hot cup of coffee. Wetting a dishcloth with warm water, she squeezed the water out and spread it over Paul's face. "Leave that on. Dad's an ER nurse and he says slow warming is the best. There's coffee in front of you, but let it cool for a few minutes. Did you get the car out?"

Paul's voice was muffled under the washcloth. "Yeah, for all the good it does us. The city plows still haven't touched this street. And I want to go and see if Gracie's changed her mind."

"If they've heard that recording, I highly doubt it. Paul they're going to be hugely p— *upset*. You know that as well as I do."

"Maybe so. But radio stations are really interested in getting more CDs of her singing. Oh, man, my nose is tingling!"

"Leave that on!" Melody ran to the kitchen and wet a second dishcloth with warm water. Hurrying back to the living room, she took off the first cloth, replacing it with the second. "So, if we can go to the community with news that radio stations are so interested in her, do you think they'll change their mind?"

"God, that feels good! I hope they'll be more willing to listen." Hearing a low rumbling sound in the distance, Paul pulled the top of the cloth down and moved to the window. Looking in the direction where the noise came from, he gasped. "The plow!" He continued holding the cloth over his nose and the lower half of his face as he watched. Because everyone had been surprised at the ferocity of the storm, they hadn't been able to move their cars.

"Paul, it's only going down the middle of the street. And throwing snow back on all the cars!"

Paul had just seen the same thing. Dropping the moist cloth, he began swearing and wishing the worst happenings on the plow driver. "You're going out there with me. I'm not doing the rest of that alone."

"Fine. But remember—you told me to stay inside when you started this work." In the kitchen, she looked for something she could warm in the microwave. "Soup. Canned pasta. Hot cereal. Oooh! These meals!" Checking the expiration dates on several non-perishable meals she'd just come across in the cabinet. "I'll make these."

Paul, smelling the scent of food cooking, wondered what Melody had found. Wandering into the kitchen, he removed the now-cold cloth and spread it over the sink. "Smells good. What did you find?"

"Microwavable meals in the cabinet. They're still good. There's turkey with fixings and meatloaf."

"Definitely meatloaf." Paul felt happier now that he knew they'd be eating something hot. "Listen, as soon as we can move the car, we'll go to the store."

Recognizing the gesture as one of goodwill and peace, Melody smiled. "Thanks. It'll be good to be able to eat fresh foods!"

᛫

After shoveling the snow back off the car, Paul managed to pull it out of the space it had been parked in. Gesturing to Melody, he sighed. "From now on, we park this thing inside the garage. I really don't want to go through this again. How does my nose look?"

"Pink. You'll live, nose and all. Yeah, while remembering what level the car is parked on is a pain, this is even more so." Melody pulled up her shopping list on her iPhone. "We need a lot. Pretty much everything in the freezer and fridge went bad." She shuddered delicately at the memory of tossing the items while holding her nose and trying not to gag or vomit.

"Yeah. Priorities. I'm starved again. Want to get something to eat before we hit the store?"

"Yeah." Melody's stomach grumbled.

On their way to Target, Paul tapped the steering wheel after making a decision. "Weather permitting, we're going to go to Crawford County on Saturday. I don't want to make the mistake of dropping in on a church service again."

"You actually looked like you were enjoying yourself, you know."

"Good acting job. I was shivering in my boots. I thought we'd get hit or beat up or something."

"Paul. Remember our research. They don't believe in fighting, war or violence." Melody's voice was dry.

That Saturday dawned very cold, windy and sunny. Jon, looking at the sky in all directions, sighed as he spotted a far-off bank of clouds. Hurrying back inside after taking care of the livestock, he spoke. "We'd better hurry after breakfast. I think another storm is coming in."

Abigail sighed. "And it's not even Christmas. Gracie, if you had plans for tonight, you'd better cancel them. I don't want you caught in a bad storm."

"Can we stop at the Lapp house, then? I need to let Abe know, although he probably saw the same clouds you saw, Daed."

"Ya, but don't take too long. I want to get to town, get our research and get home fast."

A s it turned out, the trip to the library took longer than the family anticipated. The librarian assisting them found a mother lode of information and sent several internet pages to the printer. "Mister Troyer, your bill is going to be kind of hefty." She picked up a thick sheaf of pages. "I'll staple them and put them into a couple envelopes for you."

"Denki. How much will I owe?"

The librarian sighed, totaling the fees per page on a calculator. "Including tax, over ten dollars."

"That's no problem. I'd rather have the information and be a little lighter in my wallet. By the way, is there anyone here we can speak to about someone who's bothering our family? My daughter, specifically."

The librarian looked up, her eyes wide. "That would be Missus Newton. She's in that office there, right next to the children's section."

"Thank you." Jon paid the fee and gripped two mailing envelopes, heavy with pages. "Let's go see Missus Newton." Knocking on the head librarian's office door, Jon let the woman know she had visitors.

"How may I help you? Please come in. Coffee or hot tea?"

"Coffee for all of us, I think. Thank you." Jon sat

down and wondered where to start. He sighed. "We Amish don't believe in violence, nor do we like to rely on your law enforcement. But we may be forced to do so, if two people don't start leaving our daughter alone." He explained the entire situation to Mrs. Newton. "So, they got a recording of Gracie's humming. And got it put on the radio! All we want is for them to leave her and us alone."

Mrs. Newton listened carefully, nodding on occasion. When Jon finished speaking, she looked at her notes. "Because you don't hold with taking this problem to law enforcement, you probably also don't like the idea of relying on the legal system, right?"

"No, ma'am. We can't. Is it possible for us to get help from you on the internet? We can't use it, according to our Ordnung."

Mrs. Newton smiled. "Well, it's a good thing I just finished working on my holiday project, isn't it? I'll look up what you need. What, specifically is it you're seeking?"

"Abigail? You can explain it better."

"Missus Newton, my daughter and I were talking the other evening. Because we can't use some of your resources, we figured we would try to learn as much as we can about how the entertainment world works. You see, two people who came into our community heard her singing. They want her to compete in a national talent competition, which she can't do. And now, they won't leave her alone. One of them even recorded her humming, without her knowledge. And now it's been all over the radio. And we just want it to stop."

Mrs. Newton's eyes widened. This was the only show of shock she made. "Are you talking about *The Country's Most Talented*?" At Abigail's quiet nod, she went on. "And, I hope you won't be angered, but I believe I heard the recordings you mentioned. Do they call you the Amish Songbird?"

Gracie blushed deeply. Looking down, she nodded. "I was shopping in a store in town. I didn't know he was there recording me. I promised myself and our deacon that I wouldn't sing or even hum, but I forgot. And, as I was picking the things I needed, I started just humming hymns under my breath. And somehow, he recorded me. We found out when my boyfriend heard my voice on the radio in an Englisch store."

"And, before the new storm comes in, we need to have as much information as possible so we can make plans about what to do."

"Storm? I didn't hear anything, other than winds were going to pick up and it was going to get even colder!" Mrs. Newton didn't look pleased.

"Ma'am, I saw clouds far off to the northeast.

They're probably moving in this direction. And they look like snow clouds, too."

"I swear, I'm going to move to Florida. Or New Mexico!"

"Ya, the idea is tempting."

"Well, let's get busy. I'm going to send someone out to look to the northeast and let me know what it looks like. I'm in charge today, so if we need to close early, then forewarned is forearmed." Pulling her keyboard closer, Mrs. Newton got busy, looking up information on how reality competitions were usually set up. As she did, she whispered quietly under her breath, stopping only when one of the young library assistants came into her office and confirmed what Jon had told her. "Okay, Kayla, thanks. Go ahead and finish what you were assigned. Just get as far as you can, because it looks like if the weather turns again, I'm closing early. Mister Troyer, would you be willing to go outside and gauge how much closer those clouds are?"

"Gladly." Jon sprang up and, once outside, saw that the clouds had definitely moved closer. It was also colder than it had been when they got to the library. Shivering, he sighed and went back inside. "Missus Newton, the clouds have half covered the sky. It may snow by early this evening."

"Thank you. I'll be watching the weather from in

here. In the meantime, I have found quite a bit of information for you. I'm going to look up what these types of reality shows do in the instance of an Amish contestant. Have you ever heard of a show called *Breaking Amish*?"

CHAPTER 7

Both Abigail and Jon shook their heads. Gracie had a quizzical expression on her face. "Ya, I have. But I've heard that what those kids do completely goes against anything Amish. How—?"

"Gracie, it's my understanding that the *actors* on that show aren't really Amish. It's really a poor representation of your culture and beliefs." Mrs. Newton turned back to her computer, looking for search hits about Amish contestants. "Okay, it's as I thought. If it's not on Google or Bing, it hasn't been widely discussed. Gracie, you're in the middle of unknown territory. You're going to have to rely heavily on your elders and parents as you decide what to do."

Gracie sighed, strongly disappointed. She had been so hoping that the internet would give her a badly needed answer. "Missus Newton, thank you very much. I had been praying that there would be information that I could use in dealing with the Wilsons." Her voice was low and disappointed.

"I know you'll probably say 'no' to this, but your only recourse may be taking them to court for harassing you and for stealing your voice. Hold on." Before she turned back to her keyboard, Mrs. Newton looked outside, noting that the clouds now covered most of the sky. "We don't have very much time, so I'll find what I'm thinking of quickly. Copyright law…" Her fingers flew quickly over the keys.

Jon watched as a web page popped up on the screen. His eyes flicked to the deepening clouds, which seemed to be an opalescent gray.

"Okay, this is what I was thinking about. He stole your voice without your consent. The U.S. Copyright office takes a dim view of property being taken without the owner's permission or knowledge. Gracie, your voice is your property. By secretly recording you, Mister Wilson violated our copyright laws. Here's one more document. I would strongly suggest you talk to your elders about this and let them know, if you're okay with it, that you'd like to let the Wilsons know you're thinking of filing a lawsuit in federal court. Now, you don't actually have to do that. Just the promise may make him back off."

Everyone's eyes widened. "Denki, Missus Newton. We'll take this home so you can close and get your employees home. Denki." Jon shook Mrs. Newton's hand and led his family outside.

"Oooh! It's gotten much colder! And windier!" Abigail pulled her thick wool scarf over the lower half of her face. Gracie did the same as Jon pulled his collar up over his cheeks.

❦

A s the storm was approaching Crawford County, Paul and Melody were on the expressway, trying to reach the sprawling Amish community. "Paul! Those are snow clouds!"

Paul huffed out a sigh. "I'm turning back. We aren't getting stuck here." Pulling off the road, he made a fast U-turn as soon as it was safe. Just as they were reaching the outskirts of Philadelphia, the snow started falling lazily. Less than five minutes later, the flakes were huge and falling much faster. Paul turned the windshield wipers on high, switching the heater to "defrost" as well. Ten minutes later, they pulled into their parking garage. As they were getting out of the car, Paul spoke, his voice shaky. "Melody, thanks for noticing that. I don't know that we'd have been able to make it much farther."

"Welcome. I just wonder if this kind of weather is normal for here."

Another couple passed them, laden down with plastic and canvas shopping bags. "No, it isn't. It's going to be a terrible year for snowstorms. I hope you're stocked up with nonperishable foods, because we may lose power again."

Melody, gripping her coat tightly around her, sighed. "Not again."

In Crawford County, everyone in the Amish community was ready for this storm. They ensured they had plentiful supplies of food and gas for their generators. They pulled extra stocks of oil for their lamps out and made sure those were nearby.

In the Troyer home, Gracie finished reading the information on copyright infringement. Washing her hands, she started dinner, knowing they would have to eat hot and store the rest of the food in case the storm was a long one. "Mamm? Do you want us to have extra for leftovers? I'm about to brown the ground beef for spaghetti."

"Definitely! Make extra sauce so we can have

lasagna and even a macaroni and meat casserole. What did you find out about that copyright law?"

"Not that I know much about the law, but it looks like Missus Newton was right. Paul Wilson stole my voice, my property, if that's okay to say."

"Ya, it is okay."

"Gracie, would you please help me with the livestock? I want to get finished before the snow starts falling." Jon stopped in the kitchen.

"Ya. Let me get my jacket and boots." She handed the long-handled wooden spoon to her mamm. Hurrying to the barn with Jon, she was glad he'd kept the clothesline tied between the house and barn. Gasping at the bitter air, she buried her nose and face in the top of her jacket.

"You give them feed and I'll add water to their buckets. And I hope it won't freeze."

"Put piles of hay around the buckets for insulation. I heard that from 'Horsey' Hoffstetter."

"Ah, ya, I remember that! And the livestock can eat it as well."

Quickly, Jon and Gracie finished taking care of the livestock. As it turned out, they were not quick enough. When they left the barn and locked it, the snow was falling—large, wet snowflakes dimming the view.

"Hurry! Give me your hand!" Jon reached behind him, grabbing Gracie's smaller hand.

All through the Amish community, other families were doing the same, praying their livestock would be able to get through the storm.

⊛

In the Wilson's townhouse, Paul anxiously looked over their stocks of food, both perishable and otherwise. "Man, I hope we bought enough. That snow looks wet and heavy."

Melody dragged a step stool into the kitchen. Reaching into the cabinets, she rearranged boxes and cans of food. "I'm putting the nonperishable stuff that doesn't have to be heated to the front. We'll use this food first before the power goes, if that happens." As it was arranged, the food that needed heating, such as soups or canned pastas, was all in one cabinet. Canned fruits and veggies were in another. "Oh, I nearly forgot! Paul, please get the ice chests from the storage room." She pulled two large bags of ice from the freezer. "I'm not going to do it now, but if the power goes, I'm going to put this ice in the chests so hopefully, we'll lose less food this time."

In answer, Paul set the ice chests in a corner of the large kitchen. "I'm starving. Want some chips?'"

"Yes. I might as well start eating now, because I don't want to be reaching for food if we can't use the fridge or stove."

The storm blew for nearly four days. By the time it blew itself out, only isolated areas of the city had lost power from the accumulation of heavy snow on power lines. Melody and Paul were some of the luckier few. Their electricity kept flowing, making their lives easier as they waited for the storm to end.

❦

Gracie came into the house, shivering and stomping the snow off her boots. "It's still real windy and cold out there, Mamm. At least the livestock are fed and watered."

"Here, drink this. It's chai tea, a recipe I got from the library."

Sniffing the fragrant tea, Gracie hummed her appreciation. She took a cautious sip. "It's delicious!" A thought occurred to her. "Mamm, what are we going to do with all the baked goods we can't sell tomorrow? It's market day."

Abigail sighed. "Freeze what can be frozen and

keep an eye on the rest to make sure we can throw out anything that's going bad."

"This storm is bad timing." Gracie stared outside as she drank her hot tea.

"How deep is the snow?"

"For me, knee-deep."

"Girl, go and change your shoes and stockings right now!" Abigail felt the bottom of Gracie's dress. "Change your dress while you're at it."

Jon walked in as Gracie was hurrying for the stairs.

"Husband, change your wet clothing. When you come down, we'll have some tea and cookies."

Downstairs again, Gracie gasped. "Mamm, are you using the cookies we were going to sell?"

"Ya. We may as well eat them. We can replace them next week and pray that we'll have market day."

"This puts paid to raising the bakery this week-end. It may also force cancellation of meeting services on Sunday." Jon loved the spicy tea. "What is this tea? It's delicious and it helps warm me up!"

"Denki. I found the recipe in the library while you were getting the information we were wanting."

"Please keep making it. I love it." Jon said.

Abigail smiled.

"Mamm, what are we making for supper?"

Abigail gestured to the counter. "Homemade chicken soup. We need to stay warm."

This reminded Paul to put more wood on the fire in the living room fireplace.

That night, after supper, the family continued to read the documents they had gotten at the library. As they read, they discussed what they were learning. "It looks like there's really no set policy for working with members of Anabaptist sects." Jon frowned. "That could lead to abuses of our faith and practices."

"So, this show could do whatever it wanted with me. Nee. I won't put myself in that position." Gracie's decision was reinforced in her mind.

"Ya. There's no need to put your soul or your membership here in danger. If the Wilsons or the people who own these shows can't learn to understand our beliefs, then we don't need to mess with them."

"Gracie, what did you learn from this copyright paper?" Jon was reading it carefully now.

Gracie looked up at a loud shriek of wind outside. She grimaced, grateful they were inside. "Paul Wilson did violate that law. By recording me without my knowledge, let alone permission. He violated a federal law. I think we should talk to Deacon Bontrager when this storm ends. I want his permission to threaten the Wilsons with a federal lawsuit. As far as I'm concerned, if they don't know we don't use the court system, then I should be able to let them know they broke that law. If they don't know about us and they don't bother to learn about us, that's just desserts to me."

Jon grinned. His little spitfire was back! "Ya, we do need to talk to him. We'll put these papers away so he and the other elders can read them. That way, everyone has the same understanding. And ya, I do think you should threaten them. They don't have to know we're not going to follow through."

Gracie's smile was one of relief.

***

I n the Lapp home, Ben read some of the information he and Abe had gotten. As he finished each article, he passed them over to Abe.

Abe's face was a show in distaste. "It looks to me like these shows take advantage of contestants' desire to win lots of money. They show these people at their worst. I don't want Gracie exposed to that."

"I agree." Ben took a long swig of coffee and continued to read. "Here, it says that contestants from some religious groups are at a bigger disadvantage. Their example here is a little girl from a very strict faith. They wanted her to abandon her practices about modest clothing. All so she could wear something revealing."

"No way. Gracie wouldn't agree to that. Contract or not, she would leave the show."

"Ach, and here's how they deal with that. They add a clause to their contracts. If contestants leave before they are eliminated—nice word, by the way—then they are made to pay a huge penalty."

Abe's eyes widened. *Thank Gott Gracie hasn't wanted to go on that show.*

I n Philadelphia, Paul was dreaming about the show. Gracie was singing a song, wearing not her Plain clothing, but a regular dress. Her hair was combed into a simple ponytail. As she finished her song in his dream, waiting for the judges' reactions, a loud *boom* reverberated through the room, waking Paul, Melody and other residents of the townhouse complex.

Shaking the sleep out of his eyes, Paul slipped into a heavy robe and hurried into the living room. Not seeing any damage, he was about to return to bed. It was still very early, and he wanted to sleep.

Instead, he heard smaller sounds coming from the north end of the complex. Looking out the window, he wiped it clean of condensation. Seeing a large tree that was now uprooted from the soil and accumulated snow, he gasped. The tree was now leaning inside that townhouse.

"What's that noise?" Melody shuffled into the room, holding her robe shut with one hand and rubbing her eyes with the other.

"I'm glad we decided on this townhouse and not that one. That big old pine tree just got uprooted by the winds. And it's fallen into that townhouse!"

Melody gasped, her eyes widening. She moved Paul aside and twisted her neck to look at the scene. "My God! People are coming out, just climbing over the tree. See if we have service and call 911. We can at least report this."

Paul closed his eyes in relief. The towers were still working. "Yes, Philadelphia, please. I live in a townhouse complex on Spring Garden. A large pine was just uprooted by the wind and it's fallen into a townhouse on the north end of the complex. People are leaving that apartment, so I'm not sure about injuries, so you might want to have ambulances as well."

"Thank you. What is your name?"

"Paul Wilson, W-i-l-s-o-n."

Number?"

Paul gave his number. It's a cell."

"And the exact address?"

"332 Spring Garden."

"Thank you. Help is on the way."

Paul hung up. "Okay, we've done all we can. Let's go back to bed."

By the time Paul and Melody got up, they were filled in on the events of that morning. "Thanks, man."

"Hey, why weren't you out there, helping people to get out of that townhouse? The gas lines were in danger of breaking! I think you were the only ones not out there."

Paul took offense to the implied accusation. "Hey! I called 911 and reported it! I fulfilled our responsibility!"

"Fft! I'm glad we don't know who you are. You're self-centered." The young man turned on his heel and strode away.

CHAPTER 8

Paul turned toward Melody, his posture an elaborate display of his hurt feelings. "What was all that about? We did our responsibility and got emergency crews out here!"

"He must be some kind of crunchy dude. You know, kind of a 'back to the earth' hippie type."

"Yeah, it's not like we had the tools to help evacuate people or shut that leak off, y'know?" By now, Paul was trying hard to convince himself that he wasn't self-centered. It wasn't working. As the morning wore on, the sick self-knowledge and the storm's stubborn refusal to leave made him short-tempered and snappish.

Melody, having received a snapped out retort, backed off and let Paul stew in his bad mood. She retreated to a steamy romance novel, curling up on the love seat in the dining room.

⚜

Back in Crawford County, Deacon Bontrager braved the icy roads so he could go and visit the Troyer family. Inside their home, he removed his hat, jacket and gloves. "Ya, coffee would be extremely welcome. I came here because I believe we've reached an inevitable place with the Wilsons and that show. I wanted to discuss it with you before they can come back here and take advantage of you."

Jon got a sinking feeling in his stomach. Setting his coffee mug down, he questioned the deacon. "In what way?"

Gracie and Abigail, hearing the apprehension in Jon's voice, sat down with the men.

The deacon sighed, a long, troubled sound. "Gracie, your voice is already out there. No doubt, you and your parents have been using your time wisely during this storm. What have you discussed?"

Gracie explained their trip to the library, seeking information on reality shows, treatment of the Amish on television and even the plan to promise, but not carry through, a lawsuit for the copyright infringement.

"Hmmm. Mmmm. Ya." The deacon stroked his long, graying beard as he thought. "It might work. Then again, the Wilsons are probably much better versed in the law than we are. If you were forced to go through with your promise, Jon, you would have to travel all the way to Philadelphia, to the federal courthouse there to file paperwork. And that goes against our beliefs."

Jon had been troubled by the same thought. Setting his mug down, he grimaced. "Ya, so I figured. I don't want Gracie or Abigail to get in trouble with the elders or community. Let's hear your thoughts." He didn't have to follow up with, *But there's no guarantee that we'll agree to them.*

Again, the deacon sighed. "Gracie, I've heard those recordings several times whenever I've gone to town. You're out there and people are asking to hear the 'Amish Songbird,' when they request songs to be played. You're not only on the religious radio stations, but you're also on the mainstream ones— those that play rock, country and pop. Mister Wilson set something into motion that just cannot be stopped, child. I think you're going to have to agree to be on the show."

He raised a hand quickly to forestall the inevitable refusals and protests. "I've been thinking long and hard about this. We don't know how to find the Wilsons. We don't know their phone number or even how to contact that show. We'll have to wait for them to come to us. And we are going to have to tell them that we will allow you to take part in this. Under *very* strict circumstances. You aren't yet eighteen, so your parents would have to sign a contract pertaining to those circumstances. They, and you, would be legally bound to carry out the terms of that contract. But I believe we can set conditions that protect your soul and your position here in the community.

"Now, to those conditions. Jon, Abigail, I think you'll at least find them agreeable." The deacon pulled a sheet of paper out of his jacket pocket, unfolded it and straightened it with his hands. Whirling it around so everyone could read it, he gave them the time they needed to do so.

As Gracie read it, she was stunned. *Hide Gracie Troyer's face... never allow her face to be shown on television or in print... keep reporters and fans from taking pictures of her face... respect the Amish rule against 'graven images,' or pictures of Gracie Troyer's face.* Feeling stunned and a little bit sick, Gracie looked at her parents. Their expressions were similar.

Jon spoke first. "Well, that certainly protects her ability to obey the Ordnung and Bible. But... Gracie, what do you think?"

Now, it was Gracie who sighed. "It looks like my life is about to change. In a big way. If this gets the Wilsons to stop pestering me, I guess I can go along with it. Now, I just need to find out how this show in particular is run."

Jon buried his face in his hands, ruing the day that the Wilsons had come to their community. "Deacon, can we all pray about this first before we make a final decision?"

"Of course! I wouldn't ask you to make a decision of this nature without prayer." Here, everyone quieted, closed their eyes and entered into prayer, asking for wisdom and guidance in making such a significant decision.

Gracie's heart thumped as she listened for guidance. As though from across the house, she heard a tiny voice. *You don't light a candle and hide it under a bushel. Instead, put it on a candlestick so everyone may receive its light. Let your light shine before men so they may see your good works and glorify your Lord, who is in Heaven.* Covering her mouth tightly with her hands, she looked up, her eyes widened.

Jon and Abigail heard the same Bible verse. Jon cleared his throat and spoke. "Matthew, Chapter 5, verses fifteen and sixteen."

Abigail closed her eyes. Her hands trembled slightly. "I heard the same thing."

"Ya. That's what brought me over here when I was praying about your situation. Gracie, did you hear anything?" Deacon Eli's wise eyes rested on Gracie's pale face.

"Ya, I..." she cleared her throat. "I heard the same thing."

"Ya. It appears that Gott Himself may have sent two of the most unlikely of messengers. He wants you, Gracie, to appear on this show. Whether you'll win or not, I don't know. But the next time they show up here, indicate to them that with those conditions in my note, you'll appear on the show." He grinned, producing a CD of rock-style hymns. "And the next time you see Abe Lapp, play these. I think you'll need to learn them for this show."

Gracie blushed. She knew she wasn't in trouble because of her status in rumspringa. "Deacon, I also want to ask about the schedule of shows, should I be selected to win. I do know that several contestants are approved to move to higher levels. They appear in later shows while the program is on the air. The other contestants are either required to perform and try to save themselves a spot, or they outright lose and go back home. And there are sure to be many more contestants whose voices are much better than mine. After all, I'm not trained in voice."

"Gut girl. Keep a level head on you. I have no worries about that. Stay humble."

Gracie smiled. Her lips trembled with fear and emotion.

Abigail set her hand on Gracie's. "Well, daughter, it looks like we're going to have to make new dresses, caps and aprons for you to compete. Your dresses are still in gut condition, but our little songbird will have to appear on television in dresses that befit the occasion." Her smile was also tremulous as she tried to keep tears from falling.

"The first day that it's okay to be on the road, we'll go to our store and get fabric. I'm thinking burgundy, dark green and royal blue."

"Exactly. You will maintain your modesty and Plain appearance." Jon had set his imprimatur on the new direction of the family's path.

The deacon rose. "Denki for understanding and not throwing me out on my backside. I want to make sure Gracie is protected as much as possible while she's competing. Oh, that's another thing. Competition. Don't let it twist your soul. Compete honestly and with love for your fellow competitors."

"Ya. I will."

Paul, lying next to Melody one morning, woke, puzzled by a faint sound he kept hearing. He squinted against bright sunlight. That was his first clue. Then, he heard the sound again. *Plink. Drip. Plink. Plonk. Plink.* Putting the sunlight together with the faint noises, he threw the blankets back, not noticing he'd uncovered Melody. Bounding out of bed, he didn't even hear her cry of protest. "Melody! It's sunny and the snow is melting!"

Melody, chilled by having the blankets tossed off her, stopped protesting. "What? Are you saying…?"

"Yes! We might be able to get out of here! Go to Crawford County!"

"Yeah. That and a trip to the store for more food!" Grabbing a warm robe, Melody gestured toward the kitchen. "Come on. We didn't lose electricity, so let's make a hot breakfast, clean up and see if we can drive."

"Yeah, okay. I also want to make a trip back to the Amish. See if maybe Gracie or her parents have changed their minds."

The couple made eggs and bacon, tossed the dishes into the dishwasher, and then groomed themselves. Making sure they had their debit and credit cards, phones and other necessities, they left. After returning home from the store, they debated the wisdom of a 90-minute trip north to Crawford County. Melody looked at the time. "Paul, it's already after one. We'll get there close to three and if we're going to avoid icy roads, we'll have to turn around almost immediately. I think we should wait until tomorrow morning."

Paul knew Melody was right. But he *really* needed to know if they would be able to sign Gracie. Looking at Melody's face, he realized she was right. Sighing, he shrugged. "Yeah. You're right. As soon as the roads aren't icy tomorrow morning, we take off. We don't have any meetings until Monday anyway, because of this storm."

⚜

Waiting for Abe to pick her up, Gracie paced nervously. She had to tell him about the decision she and her parents had made. She wasn't sure how he'd receive the news. Hearing his step on the porch, she whirled to grab her coat and scarf.

"What's the hurry? You're going to tell him before the two of you go anywhere." Jon's gaze was firm. He answered Abe's knock. "Abe, come in. Have some coffee while we bring you up to date."

Looking confused, Abe shed his heavy coat and black hat. At the kitchen table, he added creamer and sugar. "So…what's going on?"

Jon started to speak. He told Abe of the deacon's visit, his message for them and their decision to say 'yes' to the Wilsons. "We prayed over it and all of us got the same message. She's not to 'hide her light— her voice—under a bushel.' Instead she is supposed to share it with as many people as possible. The deacon also told us that we may be able to get some very strict concessions from the show's producers."

"What would those be?" Abe was unsettled, to say the least.

"They have to hide her face. The camera can be pointed at her, but her face can't be shown. No pictures of her face in the news. Fans can't take pictures of her face. Because we don't approve of graven images, the show will have to agree to this before we can sign anything. Or she doesn't go on the show. At all."

Abe sat back, stunned. "Gracie, how do you feel about this?"

"Stunned. Scared, a lot. But, it seems that with Gott speaking to all of us, we know now that I'm supposed to be."

"The deacon said that it seemed that, through the

most unlikely of messengers, Gott was telling us she's supposed to share her voice and Gott's love."

Abe was stunned. "Wow."

Gracie swallowed what felt like a stone in her throat. "So...are you upset?"

"Nee. I was thinking that the recording took so much steam out of our reasons to refuse."

"Ya. Even though it is copyright violation or whatever, there's not much we can do. We can't go through with any promises of suing them, not without—"

"Violating the Ordnung. Ya. They tied your hands up. So, what are you doing about this?"

"The next time they show up here, we'll meet with them and tell them 'ya,' under certain conditions. Maybe those conditions will make it impossible for them to make me compete."

Abe huffed out a sardonic laugh. "Gracie, they are desperate to get you. They would agree to walk barefoot through the Sahara desert to get you on the show." Abe's prediction was prophetic.

T he next day, after the ice on the expressway had melted, Paul and Melody were on the road as fast as they could navigate the still-slushy roads. The trip to Crawford County took them a little longer than normal. "We leave by two-thirty, Paul. I don't want to be on the road when it gets dark."

"That's fine. Hopefully, we'll make a little more progress today."

"This time, let's be honest and not lurk. Show up at their door, if we can get in. Besides, I don't want to be standing in thigh-deep snow as we snoop."

In answer, Paul shivered. "You don't need to ask twice on that." He kept driving, slowing the car until he found the house. "Looks like that new gate's actually open. I hope they're home."

Waiting at the door, Paul shivered. He wasn't sure whether that was from the cold or nerves. Hearing the *snkkk* of the lock turning in the door, he straightened up.

Gracie gasped as she opened the door. "Daed! Come here, please!"

Jon ran to the front door, not liking the note in Gracie's voice. "Wilson! What are you doing here?"

Paul raised both hands in a gesture of peace. "I don't want to p— make you angry, Mister Trayer."

"Troyer."

"What?"

"My name's Troyer, not Trayer."

Paul dragged in a cold breath of dismay. "Oh, man, I'm so sorry! Mister Troyer, we are here, honestly trying to find out if you and your family have changed your minds. We can discuss how the show works, if that'll make it easier for you."

Jon sighed, knowing he was facing a huge divide that could possibly change his family's life. Looking at the neatly dressed man and his wife, he shook his head. "Come in. Gracie, please make up some coffee. Lots of it."

CHAPTER 9

"Ya, Daed." Gracie scurried off, not sure she wanted to be in the presence of the people who had loomed over her life for the past couple months. With a shaking hand, she measured out several scoops of coffee and added water to the large coffee pot. Connecting it to the outlet, she turned it on. Reluctantly, she turned. And jumped.

Melody was standing right behind her. "Miss Troyer... Gracie, I am so sorry for what we put you through. I know this won't make up for everything, but would you please forgive us?"

Gracie slowly nodded. "Ya. I forgive you. Please, sit." She gestured to a seat next to Paul.

Once everyone was sitting, Paul licked his lips and got started. "Gracie, we both love your voice. It is…not to go overboard, but it is angelic. We behaved very badly. We know that. And…well, making that recording without your knowledge, much less your permission…um, that was unforgivable."

Gracie nodded once. "I agree. But I forgive you. I do need to let you know that we did some research. What you did in recording me without my knowledge was copyright theft. And we could sue you. But we won't, because it would violate our Ordnung."

Paul huffed out a deep breath, nearly dizzy with relief.

Abigail got up and poured five cups of steaming coffee. Setting them on the table, she turned and put creamer, milk and sugar on a small tray, which she set in the middle of the large table. She remained silent, allowing Gracie to express her fear and anger.

Gracie, sitting across from Paul and Melody, fisted her hands leaving them on top of the table.

Melody, seeing the two small fists, kept staring at them, swallowing. While she knew the Amish weren't violent, she was wondering if she was justified in fearing any sort of violence from the young girl across from her. "Gracie, we are so sorry for what we did to you." She raised her eyes to Gracie's face.

"I know. I forgive you, but I am still extremely angry with you. I was forced to change so much of my life because of you! I can't go outside our community when I'm with my friends. I'm not able to be at market to sell my baked items. Our deacon's wife has generously substituted for me. I can't even feel comfortable in my own community because of the fear that you're going to snoop on me or accost me in some way. I can't even sing in public! Do you know how hard that is when singing is my favorite way of thanking Gott for his blessings? And now? You stole my voice! Like I said, we aren't going to sue you. In our community, that would be wrong, and to me, trying to right one wrong with another wrong wouldn't solve anything."

As he listened to Gracie, Paul marveled. *How could I have ever thought we'd get one over on her, let alone her parents? She is a smart one!* He sighed. "Gracie, it's very clear that we underestimated you and your parents. Your community's leaders are also extremely wise. They've protected you, which is just what they should have done. This might sound stupid coming from me, but you are really blessed."

Gracie nodded her head, not speaking. She silently indicated that Paul should continue to speak.

"We are very sorry to have stolen your voice. We know about copyright law. Shamefully for us, we ignored it." Hearing a sharp gust of wind slapping at the kitchen window, he looked hurriedly outside. Seeing that the clouds were closer, he decided it was time to get to business. "We want to beat this storm. So we want to make a proposal to you. We really want you to compete in our show. You would have a very good chance of winning. We've seen tapes of the other contestants and, while they are good, you stand head and shoulders above them."

Seeing Jon frown, he tried to calm his worries. "No. I'm not trying to give her a swelled head or anything. She's really that good. And, that she's done this well with her voice without getting voice training? That really says a lot. Gracie... Miss Troyer... would you please reconsider? We'll give you anything you feel necessary in your contract." He felt his heart pounding as sweat collected at the back of his neck.

Gracie looked at her parents. Here it was. She licked her lips, and then took a sip of her scalding coffee. "Ya. I will. Our deacon came to talk to us earlier this week and he said that we should think and pray about changing our minds. We did and all of us got the same message. But I have to insist that your show give me certain concessions that wouldn't apply to the other contestants."

Melody pulled a small, electronic tablet from her purse. "Tell us what they are and we'll do everything we can to get them for you." She poised her hands over the small keyboard that came with the tablet.

"First, we aren't allowed to have pictures taken of our faces. From the back, ya, that's okay. If you look around our home, you'll see there are no photos of any of us. We believe these are akin to graven images, which, as in the Ten Commandments, aren't to be worshipped." She waited as Melody quickly typed.

"Okay. No photos. What does that do to your appearances when the show is being taped?"

"My face has to be blocked out somehow. Or I won't be on the show."

Melody's fingers slowed, and then stopped. "Hmmm. I don't think you've seen this before, but on news shows, when a crime victim or a witness can't have their faces shown on news stories because of a danger to them, the photographer arranges the lights so the person's face is left in the dark. Paul, can you pull something up on your phone to show them?"

"I just hope I'll be able to get... Yes, I have a signal, but it could take a few minutes for something to come up." Paul waited for a few minutes, and then finally, an image came up on the small screen. He handed the phone to Gracie, who looked carefully at the image.

"Well...the person's face is blocked out. All I see

is an outline of their head." She paused at a knock on the front door.

Jon rose. "I'll get that." Opening the door, he saw the deacon. "Come in. The Wilsons are here and we're talking now."

"Ach, gut! I want to see and hear what happens." Deacon Bontrager came in, giving his hat and coat to Jon.

"Perfect timing. Coffee?"

"Oh, ya, please! That wind is whipping up out there." The deacon sat next to Gracie.

"Deacon, we're talking now about how my face can't be shown on TV or in any photographs. There's a way the person operating the camera can block my face out with the arrangement of the lights. The only thing visible would be an outline of me. What do you think?" Gracie handed the phone to the deacon.

Like Gracie, the deacon looked at the image for several seconds. "Ya, I think this could work. Mister Wilson, she cannot *ever* have pictures or film of her face taken."

Melody resumed typing. "Okay, then we can do that. What's next?"

Gracie thought, hoping she'd remember everything.

The deacon pulled the creased sheet of paper from his coat pocket. "Here you go, Gracie."

"Denki. Okay, next. This one might be harder, depending on how well I do. Reporters and fans of the show cannot take any pictures that show my face. From the side, as long as my bonnet covers my face. Or from the back. That's the only way anyone can get a picture of me. If anyone tries otherwise or is successful, I'd have to back out of the show."

The deacon and Gracie's parents were very proud of how Gracie had taken command of the negotiations and expressed herself.

Melody blew out a long puff of air. "Yeah, that one might be harder, But I think, if we warn people ahead of time—reporters and fans—we can get them to respect it."

"Missus Wilson, that might not be so easy. We have people like you coming into our community all the time. Even though we have large signs posted everywhere—you've seen them—and we've verbally reminded visitors who *forget*, they still try to get facial pictures of children and adults. And we can't have that."

Fearing that a prize "get" was about to slip out of their hands, Melody took a large leap in her response. "Deacon—that's right?" At the deacon's solemn nod, she continued. "We still have time before the show begins taping. Our lawyers can help draft up statements that will go out to the press that will announce Gracie's place in the show. And even more, that statement can express that, under *no* circumstances can anyone take a picture of Gracie that shows her face. Like she said, profile shots or shots from the back. Gracie, would you wear the same outfits you wear here?"

"Ya...yes. I won't wear regular clothing. I'm Amish and that's not changing."

The deacon nodded in approval. "Missus Wilson, is there any way we can see a contract before the show starts?"

"Oh, of course. We're leaving soon. I've been taking notes so I can add them into the contract template we have. Once the roads are clear again, we'll bring it out here for you to sign."

Paul spoke up. "This is how I should have treated my first recording of your voice. Gracie, Mister and Missus Troyer, I'm going to have to make a video of Gracie singing. It'll comply with your rules...your Ordnung. I'll film her, using my smartphone. It'll be from the side, if there's any way you have of hiding your face. And then I'll show that in a meeting next week. Every contestant is filmed in this way, so we have an idea of what every contestant will be doing. It also goes into pre-broadcast publicity."

"Gracie, I'll get your black bonnet." Abigail

hurried upstairs, her insides trembling slightly. As she took the bonnet from the nail on the wall, her hand trembled as well. *My Gott, we are going through with this, as you said we should. Please continue to guide us.*

Gracie took the bonnet and before putting it on, she quickly smoothed her hair.

Jon moved a kitchen chair into the living room, which had the best light.

"We need to film fast before any more light disappears." Paul was nervous and excited—maybe more excited than he'd ever been before.

"Gracie, what will you sing?" Melody was curious.

"How many songs do you need?" Gracie drank some water.

"Two. One slow song and one that has a faster tempo."

"All our songs are slow. I'll sing one from our Ausbund—that's the book of hymns we use. And I'll sing "How Great Thou Art.""

"Ready when you are." Paul had set his smartphone, in video mode, onto a small tripod sitting on the kitchen table.

Gracie swallowed and licked her lips. As she nodded once, Paul pressed the record button.

Gracie sang a slow, solemn hymn from their Ausbund, as promised. It showed her wide vocal range. Next, she sang "How Great Thou Art," hoping she could remember every verse. Finally, she finished, slowly lowering her head.

Paul stopped the video. Removing the phone from the tripod, he made sure it had recorded every incandescent second of Gracie's singing. "Wow. I knew you were good, but I never realized how much range you had! We'd better go before the weather gets nasty. Can we set a tentative time to come back?"

Jon, again in command, nodded. "Ya. As long as it's on a Saturday. We do no business on Sundays. Because the weather is so unpredictable this year, we can decide on a day during the week. If the weather gets bad, don't try to come here. It's too dangerous. We'll know why you couldn't come. And, if that meeting was set up for a weekday, why don't we set it for the following Saturday?" They set a tentative date for the next Friday, weather permitting.

"Do you have a phone?" Paul was ready to enter it into his phone's contact list.

"Ya, but not inside the house. We have a phone in a small phone house. We share it with several other families. We'll hear it ring in here and go to answer. Wait for us go to outside and down the road a bit, because we don't have it connected to an answering machine." He gave their number to Paul, who punched it into his phone. "Your phone seems to do everything but milk the cows!"

Everyone laughed, releasing the tension that had built up in the house. Paul and Melody left, praying they'd beat the storm.

Inside, the deacon and Troyers looked at each other, just thinking.

ॐ

"Gawd, I hope we make it. It's really getting blustery!" Melody winced as a gust of wind shook the little car.

Paul swallowed. "We had snow in Seattle, but nothing like this." He gripped the steering wheel with sweaty hands and drove carefully. Just before they got off the expressway for their exit home, the snow started to fall. At first, it fell in slow, lazy flakes, but it quickly became a true storm, with the flakes becoming large and hitting the windshield with soft splats. Paul pulled into the parking garage with more gratitude than he'd ever felt before. "Inside!" While the storm began to blanket the city, he and Melody worked on the contract and the rough video of Gracie's audition. Finally, both were satisfied. "Well...now, we wait to go back!" Melody squealed in excitement, running around the townhouse.

❧

In Crawford County, the talking broke out at once, with everyone trying to say something. Jon waved his hands in the air, everyone stopping. "Deacon, you first."

"I just wanted to say, Gracie, you handled that with wunderbaar control and maturity. You made your points and made them well. I think, for the first time ever, they actually listened to what we had to say."

Abigail nodded. "Ya. Deacon, before you came in, she expressed her hurt and anger very well. We all respected how she did it. Even the Wilsons. They were very apologetic, asking for forgiveness."

"Ya. I'm curious to see the contract. If it doesn't have what we said it has to have, we won't sign," Jon said.

"Gut. While I think they were sincere in their regret and apologies, we would do well not to trust them too much," Abigail agreed.

"Ya, I agree! Oh! I still need to tell Abe about this! But..." Gracie looked out, seeing a few large snowflakes being buffeted by the wind. "It'll have to wait."

"I wonder how he'll react." Abigail was worried that this would put an obstacle in Gracie's and Abe's relationship,

"Mamm, he was supportive. He knows we changed our minds and why. I think he'll be another gut protection, just in case."

"Ya. I don't think they're done trying to pull fast tricks." Jon wondered if he really needed to worry.

"Jon, try not to worry. Be watchful, but leave it in Gott's hands. I'd better go before this becomes a true storm." As he drove home, the deacon wondered what would happen next.

The End.

Thank you for reading! I hope you enjoyed reading this book as I loved writing it! If so, you can grab the next book in the series here **OR you can save big and GET ALL 3 BOOKS in one collection here.** There is also a sample of the next book in the series in the next chapter.

Lastly, **if you enjoyed this book and want to continue to support my writing, please leave this book a review** to let everyone know what you thought of the series. It's the best thing you can do to keep indie authors like me writing. (And if you find something in the book that – YIKES – makes you think it deserves less than 5-stars, drop me a line at Rachel.stoltzfus@globagrafxpress.com, and I'll fix it if I can.)

All the best,

Rachel

AMISH STAR 3

With Gott's help, can she have it all?

As Gracie advances in a television talent contest, a whole new world is opened to her. Especially when it looks like she might win the thing. But when several members of her Amish community visit her in Philadelphia, she feels torn. She is called to sing, but does that means she has to leave everything behind? Can she hold onto her love while still following her dream? Or will she have to make a painful choice?

Find out in Amish Star – Book 3, the second book of the This Little Amish Light series. Amish Star – Book 3 is an uplifting, Christian romance about the power of faith and the gifts we all share.

A gain, the deacon sighed. "Gracie, I've heard those recordings several times whenever I've gone to town. You're out there and people are asking to hear the 'Amish Songbird,' when they request songs to be played. You're not only on the religious radio stations, but you're also on the mainstream ones—those that play rock, country and pop. Mister Wilson set something into motion that just cannot be stopped, child. I think you're going to have to agree to be on the show." He raised a hand quickly to forestall the inevitable refusals and protests. "I've been thinking long and hard about this. We don't know how to find the Wilsons. We don't know their phone number or even how to contact that show. We'll have to wait for them to come to us. And we are going to have to tell them that we will allow you to take part in this. Under *very* strict circumstances. You aren't yet eighteen, so your parents would have to sign a contract pertaining to those circumstances. They, and you, would be legally bound to carry out the terms of that contract. But I believe we can set conditions that protect your soul and your position here in the community.

"Now, to those conditions. Jon, Abigail, I think you'll at least find them agreeable." The deacon pulled a sheet of paper out of his jacket pocket, unfolded it and straightened it with his hands. Whirling it around so everyone could read it, he gave them the time they needed to do so.

As Gracie read it, she was stunned. *Hide Gracie Troyer's face... never allow her face to be shown on television or in print... keep reporters and fans from taking pictures of her face... respect the Amish rule against 'graven images,' or pictures of Gracie Troyer's face.* Feeling stunned and a little bit sick, Gracie looked at her parents. Their expressions were similar.

Jon spoke first. "Well, that certainly protects her ability to obey the Ordnung and Bible. But... Gracie, what do you think?"

Now, it was Gracie who sighed. "It looks like my life is about to change. In a big way. If this gets the Wilsons to stop pestering me, I guess I can go along with it. Now, I just need to find out how this show in particular is run."

Jon buried his face in his hands, ruing the day that the Wilsons had come to their community. "Deacon, can we all pray about this first before we make a final decision?"

"Of course! I wouldn't ask you to make a decision of this nature without prayer." Here, everyone quieted, closed their eyes and entered into prayer, asking for wisdom and guidance in making such a significant decision.

Gracie's heart thumped as she listened for guidance. As though from across the house, she heard a tiny voice. *You don't light a candle and hide it under a bushel. Instead, put it on a candlestick so everyone may receive its light. Let your light shine before men so they may see your good works and glorify your Lord, who is in Heaven.* Covering her mouth tightly with her hands, she looked up, her eyes widened.

Jon and Abigail heard the same Bible verse. Jon cleared his throat and spoke. "Matthew, chapter 5, verses fifteen and sixteen."

Abigail closed her eyes. Her hands trembled slightly. "I heard the same thing."

"Ya. That's what brought me over here when I was praying about your situation. Gracie, did you hear anything?" Deacon Eli's wise eyes rested on Gracie's pale face.

"Ya, I..." she cleared her throat. "I heard the same thing."

"Ya. It appears that Gott Himself may have sent two of the most unlikely of messengers. He wants you, Gracie, to appear on this show. Whether you'll win or not, I don't know. But the next time they show up here, indicate to them that, with those conditions in my note, you'll appear on the show." He grinned, producing a CD of rock-style hymns. "And the next time you see Abe Lapp, play these. I think you'll need to learn them for this show."

THANK YOU FOR READING!

I hope you enjoyed reading this book as I loved writing it! If so, **grab the next book in the series here OR you can save big and GET ALL 3 BOOKS in one collection here.**

Lastly, **if you enjoyed this book and want to continue to support my writing, please leave this book a review** to let everyone know what you thought of the series. It's the best thing you can do to keep indie authors like me writing. (And if you find something in the book that – YIKES – makes you think it deserves less than 5-stars, drop me a line at Rachel.stoltzfus@globagrafxpress.com, and I'll fix it if I can.)

All the best,
Rachel

ENJOY THIS BOOK? You can make a big difference

Reviews are the most powerful tools in my arsenal when it comes to getting attention for my books. As much as I'd love to, I don't have the financial muscle of a New York publisher. I can't take out full page ads in the newspaper or put up billboards on the highway.

(Not yet, anyway.)

But I have a blessing that is much more powerful and effective than that, and it's something those publishers would do anything to get their hands on.

A loyal and committed group of wonderful readers.

Honest reviews of my books from readers like you help bring them to the attention of other readers.

If you've enjoyed this book, I would be very grateful if you could spend just 3 minutes leaving a review (it can be as short as you like) on this book's review page.

And if, *YIKES* you find an issue in the book that makes you think it deserves less than 5-stars, send me an email at RachelStoltzfus@globalgrafx-press.com and I'll do everything I can to fix it.

Thank you so much!

Blessings,
Rachel S

A WORD FROM RACHEL

Building a relationship with my readers and sharing my love of Amish books is the very best thing about writing. For those who choose to hear from me via email, I send out alerts with details on new releases from myself and occasional alerts from Christian authors like my sister-in-law, Ruth Price, who also writes Amish fiction.

And if you sign up for my reader club, you'll get to read all of these books on me:

1. A digital copy of **Amish Country Tours**, retailing at $2.99. This is the first of the Amish Country Tours series. About the book, one reader, Angel exclaims: " Loved it, loved it, loved it!!! Another sweet story from Rachel Stoltzfus."

2. A digital copy of **Winter Storms**, retailing at $2.99. This is the first of the Winter of Faith series. About the book, Deborah Spencer raves: " I LOVED this book! Though there were central characters (and a love story), the book focuses more on the community and how it comes together to deal with the difficulties of a truly horrible winter."

3. A digital copy of **Amish Cinderella 1-2**. This is the first full book of the Amish Fairy Tales series and retails at 99c. About the book, one reader, Jianna Sandoval, explains: " Knowing well the classic "Cinderella" or rather, "Ashputtle", story by the Grimm brothers, I've do far enjoyed the creativity the author has come up with to match up the original. The details are excruciating and heart wrenching, yet I love this book all the more."

4. A digital copy of **A Lancaster Amish Home for Jacob**, the first of the bestselling Amish Home for Jacob series. This is the story of a city orphan, who after getting into a heap of trouble, is given one last chance to reform his life by living on an Amish farm. Reader Willa Hayes loved the

book, explaining: " The story is an excellent and heartfelt description of a boy who is trying to find his place in the community - either city or country - by surmounting incredible odds."

5. **False Worship 1-2**. This is the first complete arc of the False Worship series, retailing at 99c. Reader Willa Haynes recommends the book highly, explaining: " I gave this book a five star rating. It was very well written and an interesting story. Father and daughter both find happiness in their own way. I highly recommend this book."

You can get all five of these books **for free** by signing up at http://familychristianbookstore.net/Rachel-Starter.

AMISH OF PEACE VALLEY SERIES

Denial. Redemption. Love.

The Peace Valley Amish series offers a thought provoking Christian collection of books certain to bring you joy.

Book 1 - Amish Truth Be Told

Can the light of God's truth transform their community, and their husbands' hearts? Or are some secrets too painful to reveal? Read More.

Book 2 - Amish Heart and Soul

A lifetime of habit is hard to break, and for one, denying the truth will put not only his marriage, but his life, at risk. What is the price of redemption? Can there truly be peace in Peace Valley? Read More.

Book 3 - Amish Love Saves All

Can the residents of Peace Valley, working together, truly move past antiquated views in order to save themselves? Read More.

Or SAVE yourself a few bucks & GET ALL 3-BOOKS in 3-Book Boxed Set.

LANCASTER AMISH HOME FOR JACOB SERIES

Orphaned. Facing jail. An Amish home is Jacob's last chance.

The Lancaster Amish Home for Jacob series is the story of how one troubled teen learns to live and love in Amish Country.

BOOK 1: A Home for Jacob

When orphaned Philadelphia teen, Jacob Marshall is given a choice between juvie and life on an Amish farm, will he have the strength to turn his life around? Or will his past mistakes spell an end to his future? Read More.

BOOK 2: A Prayer for Jacob

Just as Jacob's life is beginning to turn around, his long, lost mother shows up and attempts to win him back. Will he chose to stay go with his biological mom back to the Englisch world that treated him so poorly or stay with his new Amish family? Read More.

BOOK 3: A Life for Jacob

When orphaned teen Jacob Marshall makes a terrible mistake, will he survive nature's wrath and truly find his place with the Amish of Lancaster County? Read More.

BOOK 4: A School for Jacob

When Jacob's Amish schoolhouse is threatened by a State teacher who wants to sacrifice their education on the altar of standardized testing, will Jacob and his friends be able to save their school, or will Jacob's attempt to help cost him his new life and home? Read More.

BOOK 5: Jacob's Vacation

When Philadelphia teen, Jacob Marshall goes on vacation to Florida with his Amish family, things soon get out of hand. Will he survive a perilous boat trip, and Sarah the perils of young love? Read More.

BOOK 6: A Love Story for Jacob

When love gets complicated for Jacob, what will it mean for his future and that of his new Amish family? Read More.

BOOK 7: A Memory for Jacob

When anger leads to a terrible accident, will orphaned Philadelphia teen, Jacob Marshall, regain the memories of his Amish life before it's too late? Read More.

BOOK 8: A Miracle for Jacob

When Jacob Marshall makes a promise far too big for him, it's going to take a miracle for him to keep his word. Will Jacob find the strength to ask for help before it's too late? Or will pride be the cause of his greatest fall? Read More.

BOOK 9: A Treasure for Jacob

When respected community leader, Old Man Dietrich, passes on, Jacob discovers that the old man has hidden a treasure worth thousands on his land. Can Jacob and his two best friends solve the mystery and find the treasure before it's too late? Or will this pursuit of wealth put Jacob in peril of losing his new Amish home? Read More.

Or save yourself a few bucks & GET ALL 9-BOOKS in the Boxed Set.

FRIENDSHIP. BETRAYAL. LOVE

SIMPLE AMISH LOVE SERIES

The Simple Amish Love 3-Book Collection is a series of Amish love stories that shows how the power of love can overcome obsession and betrayal. Join the ladies of Peace Landing as they hold onto love in Lancaster County!

BOOK 1 – Simple Amish Love
She's found love. But will a stalker end it all?

After traveling for rumspringa, Annie Fisher returns to her Amish community of Peace Landing ready to take her Kneeling Vows and find a husband. And when handsome Mark Stoltzfus wants to court with her, it seems like everything is going to plan. But when a stalker tries to ruin Annie's relationship, will she be strong enough to stand up for herself?

And will her fragile new romance survive? Read More!

BOOK 2 – Simple Amish Pleasures

A new school year. A new teacher. A hidden danger.

Newly minted Amish teacher, Annie Fisher is ready to start a new school year in Peace Landing. Having been baptized over the summer, Annie is excited to begin her life as an Amish woman. And when the Wedding season arrives, she and Mark will be married. But there is a hidden danger that threatens everything Annie wants, everything she's worked for, and everything she loves. Can Annie face it, and if she does, will it destroy her? Read More.

BOOK 3 – Simple Amish Harmony

She's in love. With the brother of the woman who betrayed her best friend.

Jenny King is elated with her new love, Jacob Lapp. But a cloud hangs over their developing relationship. Jacob's sister betrayed Jenny's best friend, Annie Fisher and has now been cast out of the church. What happens next could spell the end of Jenny's future plans, and the simple harmony of her dreams. Read More.

Or SAVE yourself a few bucks & GET ALL 3-BOOKS the Boxed Set.

A WIDOW. A NEW BUSINESS.
LOVE?

AMISH COUNTRY TOURS SERIES

Join Amish widow, Sarah Hershberger as she opens her home for a new business, her heart to a new love, and risks everything for a new future.

Book 1: Amish Country Tours

When Amish widow, Sarah Hershberger, takes the desperate step to save herself and her family from financial ruin by opening her home to Englisch tourists, will her simple decision threaten the very foundation of the community she loves? Read More.

Book 2: Amish Country Tours 2

Just as widow, Sarah Hershberger's tour business and her courtship with neighbor and widower, John Lapp, is beginning to blossom, will a bitter community elder's desire to 'put Sarah in her place' force her and her family to lose their place in the community forever? Read More.

Book 3: Amish Country Tours 3

Can widow Sarah Hershberger and her new love John Lapp stand strong in the face of lies, spies, and a final, shocking betrayal? Read More.

Or SAVE yourself a few bucks & GET ALL 3-BOOKS in the Boxed Set.

FRIENDSHIP. DANGER. COURAGE

AMISH COUNTRY QUARREL SERIES

Join best friends Mary and Rachel as they navigate danger, temptation, and the perils of love in the Amish community of Peace Landing in Books 1-4 of the Lancaster Amish Country Quarrel series. Read More!

BOOK 1 - An Amish Country Quarrel

When Mary Schrock tries to convince her best friend Rachel Troyer to leave their Amish community and move to the big city, will a simple quarrel spell the end of their friendship? Read More!

BOOK 2 – Simple Truths

When best friends, Mary Shrock and Rachel Troyer, are interviewed by an Englisch couple about their Amish lifestyle, will the simple truth put both girls, and their Amish community, in mortal peril? Read More!

BOOK 3 – Neighboring Faiths

Is love enough for Melinda Abbott to turn her back on her Englisch life and career? And if so, will the Amish community she attempted to harm ever accept her? Read More!

BOOK 4 – Courageous Faith

Before Melinda Abbott can truly embrace her future with her Amish beau, Steven Mast, will she have the courage to face the cult she broke free of in order to pull her cousin from their grasp? Read More!

Or SAVE yourself a few bucks & GET ALL 4-BOOKS in the Boxed Set.

HARDSHIP. CLASH OF WORLDS.
LOVE

WINTER OF FAITH

Join Miriam Bieler and her Amish community as they survive hardship, face encroachment from the outside world, and find love!

BOOK 1: Winter Storms

When a difficult winter leads to tragedy, will the faith of this Ephrata Amish community survive a series of storms that threaten their resolve to the core? Read More.

Book 2: Test of Faith

When Miriam Beiler, a first class quilter, narrowly avoids an accident with an Englischer who asks her for directions to a nearby high school, will this chance meeting push Miriam and her Amish community to an ultimate test of faith? Read More.

Book 3: The Wedding Season

When another suitor wants to steal John away from Miriam, who will see marriage in the upcoming wedding season? Read More.

Or SAVE yourself a few bucks & GET ALL 3-BOOKS in the Boxed Set.

A DANGEROUS LOVE. SECRETS.
TRIUMPH

FALSE WORSHIP SERIES

When Beth Zook's daed starts courting a widow with
a mysterious past, will Beth uncover this new family's secrets before she loses everything?

**SAVE yourself a few bucks &
GET ALL 4-BOOKS in the Boxed Set.**

CINDERELLA. SLEEPING
BEAUTY. SNOW WHITE

AMISH FAIRY TALES SERIES

Set in a whimsical Lancaster County of fantastic possibility grounded in strong Christian values, join sisters Ella, Zelda and Gerta as they struggle to find themselves and their places in a world fraught with peril where nothing is as it seems.

SAVE yourself a few bucks &
GET ALL 4-BOOKS in the Boxed Set.

OTHER TITLES

A Lancaster Amish Summer to Remember
When troubled teen, Luke King, is sent for the

summer to live with his uncle Hezekiah on an Amish farm, will he be able to turn his life around? And what about his growing interest in their neighbor, 16-year-old Amish neighbor Hannah Yoder, whose dreams of an English life may end up risking both of their futures? Read More.

ACKNOWLEDGMENTS

I have to thank God first and foremost for the gift of my life and the life of my family. I also have to thank my family for putting up with my crazy hours and how stressed out I can get as I approach a deadline. In addition, I must thank the ladies at Global Grafx Press for working with me to help make my books the best they can be. And last, I thank you, for taking the time to read this book. God Bless!

And if you want to keep up with new releases from me, just pop over and join my reader list here :)

ABOUT THE AUTHOR

Rachel was born and raised in Lancaster, Pennsylvania. Being a neighbor of the Mennonite community, she started writing Amish romance fiction as a way of looking at the Amish community. She wanted to present a fair and honest representation of a love that is both romantic and sweet. She hopes her readers enjoy her efforts.

You can keep up with her new releases, discounts and specials when you sign up for **Rachel's email updates list**.

Made in the USA
Monee, IL
02 August 2025

22447787R00105